The Spirits of Brady Hall

Gulf Coast Paranormal Series

Book Fourteen

By M.L. Bullock

This is a work of fiction. Names, characters, businesses, places, events, locales, and incidents are either the products of the author's imagination or used in a fictitious manner. Any resemblance to actual persons, living or dead, or actual events is purely coincidental.

Dedication

To Victoria Busby for more reasons than I can name here.

Chapter One—Bonita

Jezebel Kent is going to be furious when she finds out I'm in the running for Realtor of the year. I smiled to myself. I wasn't normally the kind of person who enjoyed making others unhappy, but Jezebel didn't hide her dislike for me. She'd spent the last year discouraging me, as a matter of fact. I got the feeling that her attitude had a lot to do with our age difference. Maybe it was my faith. Or maybe she just didn't like my accent—Jezebel was a transplant from California. Apparently, she'd been something of a Realtor rock star over there. Pretty and perky with a cute bob, Jezebel had a stunning appearance, but her heart was pure black.

Black as the ace of spades.

I had it on good authority that she hadn't even ranked in the top three for this year's annual Notable Realtor competition. *Poor Jezebel.* I rolled my eyes and shook my head at my own evil thoughts. I couldn't help but picture myself standing at the podium and accepting the plaque and the hefty bonus check while Jezebel's eyes bored into my soul from across the room. I chuckled at the scene. Such ridiculousness. Of course, it wasn't yet written in stone that I would win the coveted title, but just knowing my name was on the list made me feel good. I'd really taken a chance going to real estate school at this stage in my life, but as it turned out, the risk had been a good one. I loved it, of course, but I wasn't as prosperous as I needed to be and my divorce had hit my finances like a freight train.

And the hits kept on coming. But I wasn't going to think about that right now. I had this small victory, and that was all that mattered.

"Not yet, Bonita," I reminded myself not to gloat as I hummed and swept. Yes, everything was in place for tonight's showing. The Chivas chair and that blue glass retro lamp really worked well together. The whole place looked crisp and modern, with a hat tip to the history of the house. *You know, if I had the money to buy this place, I sure would.* If I closed my eyes and got really still, I could almost feel the crowds of people, giddy with excitement, pouring in here to see the latest play. It must have been such an exciting place—a palace of splendor. A very small palace of splendor. I could almost see the flickering gas lamps, crystal chandeliers, floral wallpaper and clean white molding.

Ah, yes. It had been and still was a beautiful place.

That was odd. I got the straight-up, déjà vu chills. Like I'd been here before, as if I'd actually come to see a play or a performance. I hadn't been alone, though. No, I'd been with someone. I paused in mid-sweep, hoping to recall some forgotten memory, but nothing came to mind.

Why should it? No, I just felt nostalgic is all. I shrugged it off. Even if I could buy this place, I wouldn't be able to keep it up. I didn't have a nest egg anymore. I certainly didn't have a wealthy partner who covered all my expenses and paid the bills. Not like Jezebel.

There you go again, Bonita. Focusing on the negative.

I put the broom back in the kitchen and checked my watch. *Oh, I'd better get busy. Open house starts soon.* I had better things to think about than a spoiled young woman who disliked me. I mean, it's not as if I hadn't tried to befriend her. Heck, I'd even proposed teaming up on a few projects, but she wasn't interested in sharing the glory—with anyone on anything.

So be it. *Fine with me. Good luck moving that house on Bellini Lane.* I had a buyer in mind, but I wasn't going to help Jezebel out. I mean, why should I? She'd made it perfectly clear that she worked alone. Again I scolded myself for fixating on my rival, but to be fair, it was for good reason. There was nothing more frustrating than talking to someone who constantly wanted to one-up you. If you had a headache, she had a migraine. If you sold a wooded lot, she sold a duplex. It was exhausting, really, and I didn't need that kind of negativity in my life. *But I swear if I win that award...*

Focus, Bonita. You have an open house today, and this isn't the time to plan your acceptance speech. I laughed at that idea. Did you give an acceptance speech at such an event? I had never been to one of those banquets before—I'd only been in real estate for two years. I never had the desire to go rub elbows with my salty peers, but this year would be something special. I'd worked hard, and I was pretty proud of myself. Enough with the sweeping. This floor was spotless. I mean, I could eat off the darn thing. *Oh, that needs a bit of dusting.*

Tick, tick.

I paused as I smoothed the linen over the small round table. That was the second time I heard that noise. I'd ignored it the first time, but for some reason, the sound gave me the heebie-jeebies. I was probably being paranoid, but what could it be? Could that be the pipes? I sure hoped not. Nothing about bad pipes came up in the house inspection. I hadn't turned the heating or air on, so it couldn't be the central system, could it?

Nope. Nothing else.

With a shrug of indifference, I went about my business and placed a pretty oval-shaped, silver tray on the welcome table and covered it with a white doily. I carefully arranged the treats on the tray, and though I hadn't actually baked these cookies, they smelled amazing and I was sure they would tempt somebody to hang around and chat.

That's what I wanted...to start a conversation. I was a good conversationalist, if I do say so myself, especially when it came to houses. And it was hard to walk away from any conversation when someone offered you cookies. Yep, I was pretty sure I'd be able to move Brady Hall in quick order. All of this downtown area had sprung to life in the past ten years, no doubt a credit to the new mayor and some savvy business owners. Maybe people just had a hankering for seeing their city improve? I couldn't be sure, but I was definitely the beneficiary of such improvements. Commerce had reawakened in downtown Mobile, and now this forgotten historical treasure was on the market. Hopefully for the last time.

Tick. Tick.

I put the empty cookie box in the crate and slid it under the table. What was that? Was there a wind blowing outside? Could it be a branch tapping against a window? I couldn't have that during the showing. I had turned on all the lights on the bottom floor, but I suddenly wished I had a flashlight with me so I could go outside to investigate. The porch light wasn't bright enough to shine around the sides of the house. Oh, why did it have to be so dark out?

What was that sound? I heard it again.

Tick.

Just one tick this time. I glanced around the room and saw nothing and no one, but I got the feeling that the sound was coming from somewhere close by. A nearby window perhaps. Was somebody tapping on the glass? The front door wasn't locked, and the windows were a little too high off the ground to imagine a person could easily tap on the glass. I guess a really tall person could reach them, but not comfortably. But why would they? I walked to the window and pulled back the curtain a little more. I'd previously swept them back with a pair of lovely gold cords complete with shimmering tassels—just like the kind of accessories one would see in a Victorian home.

Or in this case, a Victorian playhouse.

Nope. Nobody there. I stood with my hand on my hip for a moment waiting to detect the noise again, but I heard nothing else. I set up the thermos of coffee along with a few pretty, yet okay to get broken, coffee cups. With a sigh of satisfaction, I studied the room again.

Yes, everything was just like it needed to be. There were antique movie posters on the walls to remind the open house visitors that once upon a time Brady Hall had been a center for the arts. The theater hadn't been as popular or as elaborate as the Crescent Theater on Dauphin Street, but in its day it had been a thing of beauty.

These front rooms were still reminiscent of that time. Unfortunately, the auditorium had been gutted years ago, and instead of a stage and rows of plush chairs, there was a large empty room. A very large empty room, but it would be the perfect place for a venue of some sort. I was sure of that. Brady Hall had belonged to the utility company next door for over fifteen years. In fact, they'd torn down another structure to build their four-story office complex. At least Brady Hall had escaped the wrecking ball. I assumed they were responsible for taking out the auditorium. Whose idea had it been to put the two structures together? I couldn't say, but in my opinion that had been a horrible idea. Now that the utility company had left, it was my hope that Brady Hall would receive the recognition it deserved. Tri-State Realty already had an offer in the works for the adjoining building, but I petitioned them to separate the two; and much to my delight, I'd won.

Now I had to prove my chops and sell this "white elephant," as Jezebel referred to the old building. *Whatever, lady.* I just knew that I would sell this house; not only that, but I'd sell it to someone who would love it.

Tick. Tick. Tick.

I felt my stomach lurch as if I were in an elevator that had suddenly started to move.

What a strange sensation!

My feet began to feel cold—so cold in fact that I rubbed my shoes furiously on the vintage rug. What in the world was going on here? Maybe it was the air conditioning that kicked on. Was it possible that one of the staging crew had flicked it on and forgot to turn it off? That had to be it. *I'll check that out. That must be it.*

Even as I thought it, my feet wouldn't move. Not at all. My brain struggled to come up with a reason for my surprising immobility. Were my shoes caught on the carpet? *Why can't I move?* As I tried without success to move my feet, I heard the ticking sound again.

It wasn't coming from the window or the door but from the mirror, the antique oval-shaped mirror I'd recovered from the storeroom. It was a massive gold mirror trimmed with an intricate design; it really was too large for the front room, but something had drawn me to it.

Something I couldn't explain. Even with its dull glass and dingy frame, I just couldn't leave it behind. As far as I was concerned, it perfectly completed the look I was going for.

Even as I stared in disbelief at the mirror, a face stared back at me. My face and one other. It was beside me! I looked to my left, but there was no one in the room. I tried to run, but my feet were still frozen in place. I felt the stinging cold as it began to seep deeper into my skin and creep up my legs. With a scream of surprise, I watched as an inky black mist formed around my feet. It moved like a living thing, like conscious smoke, as it slithered its way up my legs.

"Stop! Help! Somebody!" I screamed, but there was no one to hear me. My phone was in my purse, which was on the Chivas chair, too far away for me to reach. I stared in shock at the mirror as the image became clearer. I detected a shadowy outline of a woman. She was about my height but younger. Yes, I knew she was young even though her face was obscured from my view. Her hair was light blondish-brown, and it was arranged in the once-fashionable Gibson Girl style. Sprigs of curls framed her face, but where there were supposed to be features—eyes, a nose, and a mouth—I saw nothing. Nothing except what looked like an erasure mark. It was unsettling, to say the least.

Horrified, I watched as hands reached up from the floor, hands in the shape of that undulating black fog. They reached for my legs, and I fell to the ground. The fog traveled up my body even as I screamed with all my might. Tears came quickly as I had never been so terrified—not a day in my life. I was sure I would urinate on myself. My body would not obey me at all. *Move, feet! Move!* Not even my screams had sound now.

The black mass quickly swirled over my body. It covered my abdomen and arms until it finally crept up my neck. It was going to kill me! I was sure of that! It would cover my face and smother me! I cried even harder. I remembered the face in the mirror and quickly turned my head, surprised I could move it at all. I had to get another look at the apparition. It would be impossible to see myself as I was on the ground. She wasn't there! The face was gone, but I lay frozen under the control of the black mist.

Suddenly, the face returned. Only she wasn't in the mirror but right in front of me! I lay flat on my back immobile as she hovered over me, her face inches from mine. Her golden-brown hair was perfectly arranged, and her black clothing, a long flowing dress with tattered sleeves, melded with the black mist. Were they one and the same? I couldn't reason this out. What was happening?

One thing I was certain of...today I would die. I believed that with all my heart.

Horrified, I stared up into the blurry face. Oh, but it wasn't an erasure mark now. Her eyes were very clear to me. They were like two black holes, two empty caverns of agony and hatred. And her mouth...oh, it was so much worse!

Like some sort of screeching portal, it began to open. Wide. And wider still. Would she swallow me? Shred me to pieces with her jagged teeth?

"NOOOO!" I managed to scream as I jerked my head away as forcefully as I could. Somehow I was able to move again and began to wriggle myself from her grasp.

The apparition screamed back from her cavernous mouth, "GET OUT!" And as her fetid breath assaulted my nose, her teeth snapped near my lips. And just as quickly as she'd come, she vanished.

I felt the terror oozing from my body. I was finally able to urinate.

Chapter Two—Sierra

To get a read on the building, I arrived early to the appointment. I had never been to Brady Hall prior to this case, but I'd easily gathered a few historical facts. Built in the 1880s, and later remodeled in 1907, Brady Hall began as a college for affluent young women. A complete rarity for this part of the state, at least in that time period. However, funding for the school failed early on and the building stood empty until a savvy businessman named Adeo Monterro purchased the property and invested a small sum in renovations around the turn of the twentieth century. It had been an intelligent move on his part.

The lecture hall became a venue for musical plays or theatre as it was called. In the beginning, Brady Hall only featured Monterro's works, but after a time he realized he needed the help of a more talented playwright. He conveniently met and married his wife, Elizabeth Shay, a literary genius who penned a number of plays including *Love's Blue Horizon* and *Ode to Rebecca*. There were rumors that *Ode to Rebecca* had been based on a true story, but I couldn't find so much as a copy of that play and knew nothing else about it. Apparently, the play had some shocking scenes. I'd found some mention of those shocking scenes in reviews featured in the Mobile Journal. But the people loved the play, despite its "savagery."

Strange, the things that people like.

I hadn't exhausted all my research avenues yet, though. My phone dinged, and I checked it one last time before leaving my vehicle. My mother-in-law had sent me a picture of Emily, who was smiling with a mouthful of mashed carrots and sporting her shiny new white tooth. Her happy smile brought a twinge of sadness to me. How was it that my daughter was old enough to have teeth coming in? When had time started to move so quickly? I sent a smiley face back and turned the phone on silent. At least Mrs. McBride and I had come to a kind of peaceful truce. We never talked openly about the paranormal anymore, not since the gathering shadows on her property had been banished to the neighbor's yard. She and I were friends now, though, and I didn't want to upset the apple cart with her. She loved Emily so much and was the best grandmother ever. Far better than my own mother, who rarely called and even less regularly paid visits.

Enough of the sentimentality. Focus on the task at hand. You'll be with Emily this afternoon.

I slid the paperwork back into my tote. This was certainly going to be an interesting case. Midas and Cassidy were still in Gulf Shores playing in the sand and enjoying a little time away. Cassidy's art show was going well, according to her pictures on Instagram. Cassidy had fully recovered from her surgery, but Midas continued to be ridiculously protective of her. I reminded him that Cassidy was tough—as tough as nails. If he continued to treat her like she was a porcelain doll, then he would be doing her a great disservice. Not to mention he would probably tick her off to no end. Cassidy had proven to be a valuable member of our investigative team and a good friend to me. I sent him a text to let him know that I had arrived, and he responded with a thumbs-up emoji.

Oh, ye of little words.

I shook my head and reached for my bag and keys. Two years ago, I would never have predicted such a day—investigating without Midas Demopolis. As I clutched at my bag of investigative tools, I reminded myself to shut down my abilities.

Being a medium came with its challenges, such as being "open" to the paranormal without even knowing it. Since the baby's arrival, this had happened more times than I could have guessed. I couldn't say why, but having a baby had made me more open to the spiritual world around me. That wasn't always a good thing. The last thing I wanted to do was attract a bunch of unruly ghosts to me, especially at my residence.

Joshua knew nothing about my post-baby struggles, but once in a while, things happened around our home. Like waking up in the morning to find a pile of ice on the floor in front of the freezer door. Luckily, it must have happened right before we woke up because none of the ice had melted.

I accused him of leaving the freezer going—he, in turn, accused me. We finally agreed that it was a freezer malfunction, but it happened two more times after that. And once more even after the repairman came out to assess the situation.

"Nothing is wrong with this unit, lady. I've replaced everything I can. Are you sure it's not one of your kids just having a bit of fun?" And he had the nerve to ask me this as I stood there with Emily on my hip.

"I only have one child, and as you can see, she's not walking yet. Much less tall enough to reach the freezer."

That offhand comment had ticked me off, but it got me thinking. I knew what was up. I'd known from the beginning. And one night, as I went to the kitchen in search of a snack, I caught the culprit.

A dead teenager.

A messed-up kid who, from what I gathered, had been killed in a car accident not that long ago. I tried talking to him, but he wasn't coherent. I gathered he was still in a state of inebriation, and not the alcoholic beverage kind of inebriant. This kid had been as high as a kite when he left this world. His death came quickly and with no warning. He spent half his current existence mourning his passing and the other half out of his gourd and unaware that he'd passed on.

After a few attempts at communication, I banished him from my home. It was the only way to get rid of him.

Luckily for me, he wasn't as strong as he could have been and it was a fairly simple procedure. But I hated doing it. I silently prayed that somehow, someone would eventually be able to get through to him. I didn't even know his name.

I got out of the vehicle and glanced up and down the sidewalk. Not a lot of pedestrian traffic out today, but there weren't many pretty spots on this street. Brady Hall had a small, unimpressive front yard. Besides this historical building, there was an empty utilities building for sale next door. A shabby-looking antiques store and a defunct restaurant were across the narrow street.

Uh oh. I see you. Stay over there, please, and I'll stay over here.

The ghost in the window of the antiques store scowled at me and vanished as she backed away from the glass.

I had known I was a medium since I was a small child. *Gosh, why am I being so mired in the past today?* I couldn't say, but I definitely was all up in my feels. Was it possible to have postpartum depression this late in the game?

Yes, I did remember that first ghost.

A little girl spirit who "lived" at the Greater Mobile Library. It took me six visits over the course of the summer to realize that the girl I was interacting with was actually dead. She always appeared in the same dress and wore an oversized ribbon in her hair. Her clothing wasn't white per se, but it was kind of colorless. Like a sort of gray, washed-out hue, and so was her skin.

At first, we played together quite easily; she was a nice kid, just a little strange. She didn't talk much and sometimes kept her face hidden behind a book. I didn't like those moments. But over that awakening summer, I began to realize our differences. Oh yes, she and I were very different. I just wasn't sure how at first. It's not like ghosts were a part of my vocabulary at the time. My family didn't believe in that sort of thing, and we never talked about anything remotely strange.

But after about the third visit, the Girl with the Bow began to act a little meaner, more aggressive. She scratched me, whispered constantly in my ear. She was mad at me for some reason or another. At first, our visits were enjoyable and I found her to be sweet. During later visits, she was moody and angry.

On one of her nicer days, it occurred to me that I didn't know her name. So I asked her, and she screamed it at me. So loudly and violently that I thought everyone in the library heard her.

"Virginia!" she screamed as if I were hard of hearing. I got the feeling that she was extremely frustrated with my stupidity. I realized that she'd been trying to tell me her name the whole time. I'd run from her that day, and the Girl with the Bow, Virginia, began to cry and faded away, right before my eyes. The strange thing was—as if that wasn't strange enough—I could hear the sounds of her crying long after she vanished from sight. If I closed my eyes and got very still, even to this day I could summon up those memories, and the sounds of her soft, sad crying still broke my heart. I visited the library dozens of times since my childhood, but I never saw Virginia again.

Why on earth am I thinking of that long-ago ghost?

I strolled up the sidewalk. I'd parked a little way down so I could stretch my legs and put out my "feelers." I believed the client had been telling me the truth; I could hear the fear in her voice on the phone. But it was best to go into these investigations with an open mind and to avoid coming to any conclusions about anything too early. I was doing my best to practice what I preached to the rest of the team. Although I was confident about the things I saw and felt—and sometimes smelled—I was also a damn good researcher. I tried to bring the best of both worlds into all of the Gulf Coast Paranormal investigations. But it wasn't all about me.

My husband, Joshua, knew everything there was to know about paranormal-related technology. He was the smartest guy I knew when it came to cameras and the like. Except for maybe Pete Broadus. Pete used to excel at finding new technologies, but he was long gone. Totally out of the picture, and good riddance. Who takes off and leaves their fellow investigators in the woods? What a jerk. Not to mention all that passed between us before. Nope. Not going there.

Joshua was the kind of guy who enjoyed pushing the envelope in everything he did. Fortunately for him, I discouraged his ideas about taking up parachuting from twin-engine planes. To be fair, Joshua was much more grounded than he used to be. When he wasn't spending time with our daughter or working at his "real job," as his mother described it, he was tinkering around with some new gadget that he believed would help us at Gulf Coast Paranormal. I was excited about his work not only because it would help GCP but because he loved it.

And he wasn't deliberately falling out of airplanes.

Paranormal investigation was certainly a labor of love because it sure as heck didn't pay the bills.

Luckily for me, Midas had a little nest egg stored away, and he paid me on time every week. We never charged clients for our work, so the financing was all on him. It wasn't my brilliant fundraising that kept us going. Sara, Midas' ex-girlfriend, used to do all that. She'd been amazing at drumming up funding, but I sucked at it. Sara had a lot of connections in Mobile society, more specifically the paranormally inclined society. But other than selling a few T-shirts now and then, I wasn't doing much to bring in any extra cash. I really hoped I could change that. But how?

I had no idea.

Midas was our leader, but to me, he was a big brother. That's what I called him most of the time. Big Brother knew everyone in Mobile and had the biggest heart of anyone I'd ever known. I was glad that he and Cassidy were together. She was good for him and vice versa.

Cassidy was a psychic artist who drew pictures of the dead and often times uncovered key components of our investigations. Cassidy was always one to share a painting or a sketch or drawing. Unfortunately, we wouldn't have her help on this case. I wasn't sure that she knew about Brady Hall, but I left that up to Midas. If he didn't want to tell a team member about an investigation, that was on him.

If we officially took this case, I would most likely bring in Bruce and Helen, our two most faithful part-time investigators. We would definitely have to bring on some new team members soon, though. Helen had decided to gift Dixie House to her niece, and she and Bruce were moving to Gettysburg in the fall. He had a son up there, and Bruce was particularly fond of investigating in the Gettysburg area. They would be missed, but I understood their decision. Helen's health had improved a great deal over the past few months, but she just wasn't happy investigating ghosts like she used to be, and that was a problem. I couldn't say that I blamed her—after all, she'd had a few close calls with death recently.

I stared up at the brick façade and searched not only with my physical eyes but with my spiritual ones. For a second or two, I experienced an intensely creepy sensation that I was being watched, but it did not last long and I was not able to make contact with anyone. Or anything.

There is no sense in hanging out here, Sierra Kay. You can reminisce about the past later. You've got work to do.

I remembered to smile as I walked up the steps. Sometimes my intensity came off as unfriendliness. I didn't want that, but nevertheless, it was challenging to not look like some unhappy weirdo. I remembered to lock the door of the vehicle and tapped the fob in my pocket. As I did that, I was immediately awash with bad vibes.

Yikes! I peeked over my shoulder at the antiques store, but it was definitely not coming from there. It looked like whoever owned the place had shown up. Two women were walking toward the store with armloads of items. No, not from there. This persistent "go away" feeling wasn't coming from that poor ghost. The dead lady at the antiques store might be a little territorial, as most intelligent ghosts tended to be, but she wasn't sending me this dark energy. So where was this coming from? If I had to describe it, I would use my mother-in-law's terminology:

This place had some bad juju.

I immediately began visualizing a protective white light around me and felt better in a few seconds. The outside of the building was made of red brick, but I knew this was not the original appearance. When it was built, Brady Hall had a wooden front with many odd, carved details. Scrollwork to the max. Were those letters inscribed in the woodwork? And then the veil fell and I couldn't see the house as it used to be anymore. Just the bricks and the concrete and some freshly painted iron railings.

White light, Sierra. Put your shields up, idiot!

A woman waved at me from the porch. "You must be Sierra McBride. Hi. My name is Bonita. Thanks for coming on such short notice." Bonita startled me, but I remembered to keep my composure as I stepped back into this world. She had a tidy appearance just like she stepped out of a professional businesswomen's magazine. She sported low heels, shiny pantyhose, and a fitted black suit. Her hair was cut in a short pixie style, but it suited her. If Bonita Hutchinson was going for the total-professional-no-nonsense look, then she'd definitely nailed it. Her face, while friendly, was absent of a smile, and she didn't waste any time with chitchat. "Please, come inside."

"Nice to meet you in person. Thanks." I followed her into Brady Hall and immediately knew we weren't alone.

"Helen told me about your organization. She speaks very highly of you all. I'm hoping you can help me get rid of this thing. It's dangerous, Mrs. McBride. It's not just a ghost. I don't know what it is, but I don't want it to stay here; it can't be allowed to stay. Let's be clear about that. It has to go."

"It's Sierra. Please call me Sierra." I understood she felt desperate. People in her situation often did, but we were going to take this one step at a time. I needed to make that plain to her right from the beginning. We had a certain way of doing things, and we weren't going to do them any differently in this case. I understood she was terrified, but I didn't think she was in imminent danger, and this was not her residence.

I prayed to God that Helen hadn't unknowingly misled Bonita about what we could do for her.

"I'm not sure what all Helen has shared, but I can promise you that we will do our best to find answers for you. I have to be honest, though, Bonita. Getting rid of a spirit is not always easy, and it's not always an option. But first things first, let's figure out what kind of haunting you are experiencing."

"There's more than one?" Bonita asked breathlessly as she smoothed out her jacket awkwardly.

"Yes. Lots of different kinds. Sometimes we follow up an initial meeting like this by talking to other witnesses to hear their stories. I'll walk around the property and take a look at some of the potential hotspots. I've done a little research before coming today. That's standard practice, but we'll do more research during the course of the investigation. It takes time to compile information about who or what may be responsible for the haunting. If there is a haunting."

Bonita's eyes narrowed, and she sagged slightly on the elegant couch. I sat across from her and resisted the urge to hold her hand. I couldn't offer that kind of comfort at the moment. I didn't need to confuse her energy with whatever else was in Brady Hall, and if I touched her, I certainly would.

"There is a haunting. I can promise you that. I saw the face in that mirror over there and then the other thing; it was black, like a shadow. No! Like a mist! I can't be sure, but it grabbed my legs and wouldn't let me go. First my feet and then my legs...then everything. I thought it was going to smother me."

"Go on. You didn't tell me about that, Bonita. When did this happen? You say the same day you saw the image in the mirror? That mirror?"

"Yes, that one. I'm not particularly proud of what happened after—I'm almost sixty, Sierra. I had an accident, and I haven't peed my pants since I was a toddler. I am ashamed to say it, but when that thing manhandled me, I peed on myself. Right there, on that rug. I thought I was going to die."

Bonita's body language backed up her statement. She seemed terrified.

"I see. And that was here?" I pointed to the rug in front of the couch. I didn't see any stains, but the fear in her voice was palpable. It was a damn expensive rug, that was for sure. And I couldn't be sure, but this couch looked like a Michael Amori Manor Wood Sofa. And if it was, wow. Those things were pricey. I was impressed with the beauty of the room. I got the feeling that Bonita really loved this place, felt a sense of ownership.

Hmm...That might be a problem.

That's when I heard an unusual sound, like a bowling ball rolling down bare wooden stairs. Bonita heard it too because she gripped the carved wooden arms of the sofa as I jumped to my feet. No time for any more of this interview. The spirits of Brady Hall didn't need a spokesperson.

They wanted to meet me personally.

Chapter Three—Sierra

"I know this sounds crazy, but I feel like there should be stairs right here. I don't see any stairs. You heard that sound too, right? And it was darn close." That wasn't a question—more like a statement. I was pretty good at locating the origins of phantom noises. Not as good as Joshua, but I usually got things like this right. And in my mind's eye, I saw a narrow stairway with golden and red floral carpet.

"It's true there used to be stairs here, but that's been a hundred years ago. Maybe more. They took these particular stairs out way back when G.L. Lawson bought this place in the fifties. I can't say why he did it, but they moved the staircase to over there." Bonita pointed toward the end of the hallway. We traveled down the hallway cautiously, but everything was all wrong. This was not something that happened normally, but seeing two time periods superimposed over one another was making me slightly ill. I had to pause to make sense of it all.

"I feel likc I need to get a handle on this layout. It's much bigger inside than it appears from the outside, isn't it?"

"Yes, it is." For the first time in our conversation, Bonita smiled. It was a careful smile, and there was no hiding the terror that was still in her eyes. "Just through this door is what used to be called the lecture hall and later the theater. Unfortunately, none of the original stage or chairs remains." She sighed sadly like that was the biggest crime in the world. "It's more like a big, empty warehouse in here. I'm calling it a multipurpose room because that sounds better. I am trying to sell the place as a venue. One can easily envision weddings and receptions here. Or at least I used to, but now I can't imagine selling this place. What if someone gets hurt?"

"Interesting," I said as I stepped into the large, empty room. She was right; it was kind of too vacant. Derelict. Kind of sad, despite the modern light fixtures and elegant furniture. It was as if the place had lost its identity.

"Bonita, let's just walk around and you can tell me about any feelings or experiences you had. Anything at all. Be honest. I'm not looking for validation for what I see or feel."

"Oh! You're a psychic? I didn't know that. I thought you guys were more of a science-based organization."

I remembered to smile despite Bonita's possibly wavering trust in me. "I have some abilities, yes, but I don't rely solely on them. Sometimes, what I sense gives me clues and places to start, but the investigation will move forward in the most scientific way possible. I'm just doing the preliminary walk. If we take this case, the whole team will come together to gather evidence to present to you. And possibly a solution."

"*Possibly* a solution?"

"Yes, ma'am. That's all we can offer you. I'm afraid there is no guarantee that we will be able to find anything or be able to get rid of any spirits if we do find evidence. It's just not a black-and-white science. I am sorry. I hope you're okay with that?"

Bonita thought about the question for a moment and eventually nodded her head slowly and said, "I understand. As

I don't know what I am dealing with, I can't say no. Who else will help me?"

"Has anyone else experienced anything similar to what happened to you? Anything at all?" I felt a little desperate because the energy here kept moving. I remembered to keep my game face on—I didn't want to frighten Bonita further, but man, this energy! It was intense, for sure, which could only mean it was an intelligent energy. Not a collective but multiple entities. Yes, there was more than one.

Shades of the Leaf Academy.... Nope. I'm not going there.

Why would I even think of that now? The Leaf Academy was a one-time deal. This was no maelstrom.

"I'll be honest with you, Sierra, I think people are having experiences but aren't sharing them. You have to remember that the utility board was here before and, boy, the most closed-mouth group of folks you've ever seen in your life. Casper the Ghost could confront them, and they wouldn't admit it. But I guess it wouldn't hurt if I quietly asked behind the scenes if anyone has seen anything. As far as I know, the only person who's experienced anything in this house besides me is a member of the realty company's staging crew. Her name is Britney. She's young and more open to these things than I am, or so I believe, but there's nothing to suggest that she's making any of it up. And she has evidence, a photo. It's the same apparition I saw in the mirror."

That piqued my interest. "You have a photo of an apparition? Where is it?"

"On my phone, back in the front parlor where I left my purse. That's where everything is happening—in that front room. I heard what you heard a few minutes ago, but that's the first time I've heard that particular sound. I don't know what that was. Until that day, all was quiet here. But I know I saw that face in the mirror and the black mist creeping up my legs; all of that happened in the front parlor. Maybe my decorating stirred things up? Maybe restoring this place to its original look was a bad idea?"

"Don't blame yourself, Bonita. Renovation does kick things up sometimes, but that can only happen if there's something here to begin with. And I have to say, though I probably shouldn't, this is an unusual place." We continued to walk through the old theater and toured the rest of the house.

Strangely enough, the second floor was very quiet and actually quite peaceful. It was there that I caught the scent of an old-fashioned perfume, but it only lasted a few seconds. And as far as I knew, that wasn't from my new friend.

What was that? Lemon verbena? No, something else.

I paused in the hallway to read the scent, but there was no recapturing it. I was a little saddened by that but happy that at least this floor was peaceful. It wasn't as elaborately decorated as the bottom level, but Bonita had done a great job of making it feel cozy without feeling cramped. Often times in these attempts at reproductions, I found that people liked to cram too many things into the space. In actuality, Victorian folks weren't hoarders. Not in my limited experience. People in the Victorian age kept fewer treasures than our modern culture did, but the things they did keep were often precious. Like silver-framed pictures or crystal glassware. You wouldn't find anything cheap in a middle- or upper-class Victorian home.

"Back in the day, this level was the residence. The Monterros lived here, and before that, some of the school's students and teachers called this place home."

"Interesting," I replied as we walked toward the stairs. I paused. "Is there an attic?"

Bonita thought about her answer and said, "Yes. Yes, there is, but I haven't been up there much. Would you like to see it?"

"I would."

"I'm not sure I can reach the latch, but we can give it a try." And she was right, both of us were too short of stature to reach the pull-down chain, but she gave me permission to check out the attic with the team when we came back to investigate.

"So, you *are* going to investigate? You'll take the case, then? You'll help me?"

I smiled at her confidently. "Yes. I think we should take this case." I cast a worried eye toward the attic. Yes, that was where that spirit liked to hide—no, make that spirits. A raspy voice in my ear warned me away, but I couldn't make out what it was saying. And Bonita didn't seem to hear it at all.

"How soon can you get started?"

"If everyone is available tomorrow night, then tomorrow night. I'll go back to the office today and meet with them. We'll decide what technology we're going to bring, and then I'll give you a call. How does that sound?"

"That sounds great."

Bonita and I made the circle back to the front room, and she dug in her purse to find the photograph she promised me. I'd almost forgotten about it because my energy continued to be drawn to that attic.

"Here's that picture, Sierra. I can forward it to you as well. I'm sure Britney wouldn't mind. And if you want to talk to her, just say the word and I'll make it happen. She's a really good kid, and I know she would want to help. Take a look at this."

"Wow," I said to myself as I viewed the photograph. Bonita wasn't lying, and this photograph was no joke—this was an interesting piece of evidence, for sure.

The face in the mirror wasn't a human face at all. Not a living human. It just couldn't be. This was the face of a skeleton, only it wore an elaborate hairstyle. Blondish-brown hair piled up in the Gibson Girl fashion. The hair was lovely enough, but that face! Or lack of one, I should say. I was eager to get this picture into our software and blow that sucker up. Luckily, the photo had been taken with good lighting, but it was slightly grainy and the image was off to the side at a strange angle. This wasn't a straight-on face in the mirror, and there was no picture of the person taking the photo, which gave me hope. If only Jocelyn could see this. What would she think about it? No way was this Photoshopped, but then again, I'd been fooled before. Josh would be better at picking out the telltale signs of an editing job.

"Definitely send this to me, please."

A few seconds later, I received the image in my email. And after having Bonita sign a few documents ensuring that we wouldn't be sued for anything that happened here, I left Brady Hall with an unusually high level of excitement.

With one last glance up at the attic window, I pulled away from the theater and drove straight to the Gulf Coast Paranormal office.

It was time to go to work.

Chapter Four—Midas

"What is this you're sending me, Little Sister? What am I looking at here?" I asked as I squinted at the tiny picture on my phone. I gave Cassidy a glance. Thankfully, she wasn't paying a bit of attention to what I was doing. There were interested patrons looking at her portraits, and she was very deep into conversation with one in particular.

"Put your glasses on, Midas. Are you telling me you don't see a face in the mirror?" Sierra was right, of course. I needed to start wearing my glasses more faithfully, but I'd left them in Mobile. Honestly, I wasn't even sure where I put them. There was no doubt I'd have to start using them, at least for reading. My eyesight wasn't improving—I needed to stop being so vain.

"Let me change positions and find some better lighting," I lied as I stretched the photo with my fingers to get a close-up shot of this so-called specter. "Interesting," was all I could say as I stretched the photo as far as it would go. After examining the strange, skeletal face, I quickly searched for evidence of odd shadowing. Something that would debunk this frightening image. Photos were easy to manipulate, and we'd seen our share of such attempts in the past. There was no doubt that this woman in the mirror was a terrifying sight. The reflection was black and white, but not the whole picture. There was a slight coloration or colorization to the hair of the apparition, but the face was something to behold. It was clearly meant to appear malevolent, menacing. Strange that it wasn't staring directly at the person who was taking the picture. The face stared straight ahead as if its focus was on someone else. Someone unseen. I said as much to Sierra.

"Who else was there besides the person who took this picture?"

"I didn't think to ask, but I will," Sierra answered quickly.

What a compelling image! I couldn't stop staring at it. "I would start by finding out who else was in the room. And if there was someone else, where were they standing? You know what to ask. What time of day was this? Did they feel anything unusual? Did they see the image before they took the picture, or did they only notice it afterward?"

"Okay, okay, bossy. I know how to run an investigation. I just wanted you to see the picture. I don't think it's been manipulated, but I'll definitely let Josh take a look at it."

Her mention of Photoshopping reminded me of a recent phone call with a fellow investigator and friend, Rose. She had mad skills with this kind of thing. "You know what, Sierra? I've got the perfect person to bring in on the photo. Lead the team on the ground. As you've reminded me, you know what you're doing. I'd suggest, if you were to ask me, that you try to debunk that image and have Rose run the original through her program."

"Wait a second. Rose? Oh, Ben's girlfriend?" Before Ben's death, a few years ago, she'd had a little crush on him, but he'd already met Rose and soon after Sierra met Joshua. Yeah, my cousin Ben had been totally in love with Rose. She was all he talked about. I think the feeling had been mutual. I met Rose a few times, and although we shared similar interests, namely the paranormal, she was a bit standoffish. I felt as if there was a story there, but I never uncovered it. Ben's death came as a shock to us all, and I am ashamed to say Rose and I didn't stay in contact.

I was surprised to receive a text from her a few days ago asking if there were any positions open at Gulf Coast Paranormal, or if I was interested in working with her on a few cases. She said she was passing through for a job and may stay around awhile. I couldn't imagine that she would ever really leave New Orleans, but who knew? And it's not like we weren't short-staffed. I had a file cabinet full of potential team members, but ever since Jocelyn Graves' accident, I hadn't had the heart to look through any of them.

"Yep. That's the one. She is amazing with photo technology. If there's any funny business going on, she'll figure it out. That is definitely a terrifying image. If it's legit, move forward with caution," I counseled as I stepped out of the way of a buzzed patron. The draft beer was flowing at this beachside art fair. I normally didn't imbibe, but those foamy drinks were tempting here on the sunny beach.

"Well, duh. Are you going to tell Cassidy about Brady Hall? Am I supposed to lie to her and pretend that we're not investigating? She's been texting and sending pictures of her art. I don't like being put in the middle, Midas. You know I love you, but what are you protecting her from?"

"I haven't asked you to lie, have I? Please, just do the investigation and keep me posted. Look, I have to go. Cassidy is calling me. Her paintings have been selling well. It looks like she sold one of her last pieces. We might be home sooner than I thought. I'll tell her about Brady Hall when the time is right, but I want her to enjoy herself. You know, do something she loves. For now, she needs to focus on what she's here to focus on, and that's finding people who appreciate her art."

An awkward silence passed between us. "I love you, Big Brother. I hope you know what you're doing." She hung up the phone, and I slapped a smile on my face as Cassidy waved me over to meet her new patron. In my heart, I knew what I was doing was wrong—or at least not quite right. Keeping secrets in a relationship wasn't good. They were like poisonous darts, ones that you launched at yourself. Darts that painfully struck you when you least expected it.

But I was just trying to protect Cassidy, right? It's not like I really wanted to keep her away from the world of the paranormal. Then again, that was exactly what I was doing. But could Sierra or anyone else blame me? I almost lost Cassidy on this last investigation. She'd become completely obsessed with sketching the dead at Oakleigh House—she'd been so focused on making that connection that she'd put her health at risk. Extreme risk.

No. I wasn't going to lose another team member, especially my own fiancée. Never again.

"Midas!" Cassidy said as she put her hand up to shield her eyes from the sun. She'd forgotten her sunglasses again. More like lost them. She was good at doing that, losing sunglasses. "Come meet Aretha. She's an artist too!"

I made my way across the sandy pathway and tried to lose myself in the happy world of the living. And I didn't feel bad about it. Not one bit. Well, not much anyway. At some point, I'd call Sierra back. No, I'd do one better; I would call Rose and tell her about the situation. If she was still in Mobile.

Chances were the team was being punked. But then again, there was always the slim chance that the image was real. A real apparition caught on digital film. That was a rare thing.

Yeah, I'd have to take a look at it again. I'd have to see for myself. When Cassidy wasn't around. Maybe after she went to sleep.

I smiled again as I shook Aretha's hand and pretended to listen to her talk about her work. This was going to be a long afternoon.

Chapter Five—Lynette

Adeo's fingers tugged at my corset strings, but I pushed them away playfully. We had to be practical about this. There was no time! No time for completely undressing and exploring one another's bodies. This wasn't one of those opportunities—those were far too rare. Too few and far between. More and more, Adeo sought me out for quick couplings, unemotional lovemaking, but my heart did not want to believe the truth...Adeo Monterro had no plans to leave Elizabeth. No plans to make me his wife. None at all. I didn't want it to be true! Not after everything I had done for him.

"No! Someone will find us, Adeo!" I warned him as he shoved me against the wall and kissed me ferociously. His need was great, he whispered in my ear. And then he whispered the words I was hungry to hear.

"I love you...adore you...need you...don't deny me!"

Although I would not allow him to fully undress me—the play would begin in less than an hour—I did not refuse him. I wanted him as much as he wanted me. I allowed myself to hold out desperate hope that this somehow mattered. That this physical connection mattered. As I sweated, my bun sagged in the heat. It was a warm day already, and my skin grew slick with sweat as it always did when I had an encounter with Adeo. We had fewer and fewer encounters recently, but he wasn't to blame. He loved me. He told me that regularly. Maybe not in those specific words, save only during our first few intimacies, and now, but in his deeds and actions his love was always intimated. *Our love would last forever.* That was my favorite line from *Ode to Rebecca*, and I believed they were meant for us. Every time he spoke them on that stage, his deep voice booming and musical, I knew he was speaking directly to me. Directly to my soul!

Oh, Adeo! How I love you!

As our lovemaking came to an end, my hands lingered over his face. The touch of his skin, the squareness of his jaw, the defined prickles of his sophisticated beard, all of these things I loved about him, but it was more than physical attraction. It was his soul that I longed for. I wanted to possess Adeo Monterro, as only a wife could possess her husband. Only one thing stood in my way—Elizabeth! But not for long.

"I love you, Adeo. I love you. You have to tell her, my love. We must tell her together, Adeo. It is time to do what you promised," I demanded as my heavy skirts fell and my lover cinched his pants. "You promised," I reminded him as I tugged at my corset strings and swept up the flyaway tendrils from my face. I would have to find a mirror to tidy myself and some perfume to hide the scents of our lovemaking.

"Ah, you shouldn't love me, dear Lynette. Isn't this enough, my lovely one? Aren't these moments enough? Why ruin them with such talk? We would only cause pain, and you know that Elizabeth hasn't been well for a long time. If I tell her now, while she struggles so, it will kill her. You must understand. Please, do not ruin this."

I slapped his hand away as he reached out to stroke my flaming cheek. "I am not ruining anything. No! It is not enough! Not at all! I'm not your whore, Adeo! I want what you promised! You promised that I would be your wife. That I would be yours, as your only love!"

His attitude changed immediately, as quickly as the weather during the approach of a summer storm. "People often say things they do not mean in the course of lovemaking, Lynette. You were no innocent, my dear. It is an art, this seduction. You will never be a true artist for the stage, but my, how you seduced me! Of that you should be proud, for otherwise, I would not have given you a second look. No. There is no argument, Lynette. My affection for you has run its course. I cannot harm Elizabeth..."

"You dare speak her name to me," I snarled at him.

"She is my wife, Lynette. Until the day she dies, I am her husband. In case you've forgotten, *Ode to Rebecca* is her property, her art. If she walks away, she takes it with her. She is the brilliance behind the curtain and on the stage." He slid his coat on and adjusted his collar. His dark eyes narrowed as he studied me. "It's a pity you didn't seduce Elizabeth instead. You are very much her type. I do believe she would have liked you, Lynette."

"Don't say such things to me. You can never say that. I don't believe any of this, Adeo. I don't believe what you say. Tell me you love me again. Can your love be so changeable?" I pleaded with him. From the crowded closet I could hear footsteps, high heels coming down the hall. *It must be dreamy-eyed, pale-faced Elizabeth. She wore high heels every day of her life.* I cut my eyes at the door and back at Adeo. All I had to do was cry out. All I had to do was scream, and the world would know the truth about us.

Elizabeth would know the truth.

He must have read my mind because he put his finger to his lips, the universal sign for quiet, but I had no mind to oblige him. I reached for the door as I determined to take the most unforgivable action. *Time to face the music*, I thought as I smiled at him wickedly.

He loved me. He would have no one else, but Adeo lacked the courage to do something about it. Oh, but I wasn't afraid to speak. What did I have to lose, except Adeo?

I reached for the door when suddenly he snatched my arm with one hand and clamped his other hand over my mouth. I screamed into his palm and managed to bite him, but he did not scream, nor did he let me go. Not until we both heard footsteps hurry back down the hall. He snatched his hand away and cursed at me, but I did not apologize. I wiped the blood from my mouth and stared at him mutely.

It sounded as if we weren't the only ones here on the second floor. And I could hear the music from downstairs in the orchestra pit. There would be much activity tonight as the play resumed after the short break we'd taken here at Brady Hall. Elizabeth had been ill for a few days, but unfortunately, she had recovered.

I had not given Mrs. Monterro enough of the poison to do the job. I served her the poison-laced tea on three separate occasions, but either she did not drink enough of the tea or I'd failed to measure the right amount of the poison. I was disappointed but thankful that I had not gotten caught. Technically, this had been a practice run. I regretted that it failed, but I had learned quite a bit. Elizabeth had been stronger than I believed, physically at least. She'd recovered in just a matter of days. He should know. I should tell him what I have done for him—for our love!

"You don't understand, Adeo. What I *will* do for you. Say the word, Adeo, and you will see. You will see how much I love you. With all my heart, I love you. She can be gone; I can do that." The taste of his coppery blood in my mouth strangely excited me. He was wrapping his hand with his handkerchief and swearing at me.

"I am warning you, Lynette. Stay away from Elizabeth. You weary me, girl. Our time has come to an end. It is over between us, Lynette."

"What do you mean? You can't do this! We've been together too long—too many times, Adeo—for you to say that this means nothing to you. What about all the things you have promised me? I am yours and you are mine. Remember that? No, Adeo. Elizabeth will not stand in our way. I will not allow it."

Despite my desperate words, I felt a strange sort of calm come over me. I knew what I would do. I would do what he could not. The little girl would help me. I would summon her, and she would do what I asked. Then Adeo would see reason. He would understand after it was all over. He was speaking to me now, but the words sounded strange as if he were speaking to me underwater. I laughed at the effect, uncaring that I might offend Adeo.

"Mad girl!" he muttered as he reached for the door.

"Not so mad, I think. If I were truly mad, your wife would not have risen from her bed."

And even though I didn't say it directly, something in my face—in my expression—must have revealed to Adeo the truth of what I had done. I'd been the one to cause Elizabeth's illness. He quite easily put two and two together. He grabbed me by the arms and began to shake me. Yes, I used the poison but failed! As I always failed!

"It was you—you made Elizabeth sick! How? How did you do it?"

I laughed at his stupid question. "I am only doing what you will not, my love. You promised me that I would be by your side. That she would be gone. You promised. I did it for us."

Adeo's hands fell away as he reached for the door again. He was going to leave me. Not merely the room but me! I could feel my hold on him slipping. Those savage moments of stolen lovemaking were not enough anymore. And the truth of the matter was that Adeo still loved his wife—sterile, mad Elizabeth. All this became clear to me. Very clear.

"Say it, then, coward. Say what it is you want to say and be done with it."

My hands gripped the table behind me as I felt the world begin to collapse around me.

"We are through, Lynette. There will be no more of this, and we will not speak of any of what you have done. You should leave the theater. I never want to see you again." He opened the door and slipped outside, closing the door behind him.

Suddenly, Brady Hall came to life. There were people everywhere. People upstairs, downstairs, all around, and they were preparing for tonight's performance. Mrs. Monterro would take her place again in *Ode to Rebecca*. As her understudy, I was no longer needed, and as Adeo's mistress, I was cast aside.

I had been a complete fool to believe Adeo. He had never planned to leave Elizabeth—I could see that now—but if he thought that I was going to lie down and let him have his way, that I would let him take what he wanted and not demand payment, then he was very mistaken. This would be the last time he felt my flesh beneath his, the last time I would declare my love to him or to any man, the last time we spoke in such an intimate fashion, but this was far from over.

I still had every intention of destroying Elizabeth; she had done her very best to destroy me by speaking negatively of me at every opportunity, and I would certainly repay her the favor. Yes, indeed I would. Oh, but I had a new target now.

Not just Elizabeth. Adeo Monterro would die too. In those few seconds, as I paused at the door and waited to join the troupe again, I knew exactly how I would accomplish such a thing. No, I wasn't going to leave Brady Hall. I would pretend to make peace with Adeo when his mood had calmed a bit. I would assure him that all was well and that we needn't fuss and fight. I would wait.

And I knew exactly how I would get my ultimate revenge.

I hated Elizabeth, to be sure, but I now hated Adeo Monterro much more. He would die in a suitable manner, and not by my hand but more elegantly. He had no idea how clever I could be. No idea at all. I rubbed my tongue over the lingering blood on my lips and, strangely enough, savored the taste of it. I never knew I had a taste for blood.

But I did.

Soon, I decided, *I would have all the blood I wanted.*

Chapter Six—Sierra

"Gulf Coast Paranormal," I answered the phone without glancing at the caller ID. "This is Sierra speaking. May I help you?" I paused as I normally did as I flipped through the packing checklist that Joshua handed me. He wasn't joking around on this investigation, but I thought we were bringing way too much equipment for Brady Hall. Did we really need to lug in two SLS machines? These were my thoughts as I waited for the caller to speak, but there was no one there. Nothing but dead air. I glanced at the caller ID expecting to see a Robocall number, but Peter Broadus' name blinked on the screen.

"Pete? Are you there?" I asked, silently praying that he butt-dialed me because I was not prepared to have a conversation with a former friend and team member.

"I'm here. Sierra? Is that you? Are you busy? Can we talk a minute?"

I tossed the paperwork on my desk and plunked down in the chair. Joshua passed by the door, and I waved for him to come in. I hit the speaker button on the phone and put the receiver on the cradle as quietly as possible. With my finger to my lips, I waved at Joshua to close the door so we could guarantee our privacy. I wasn't sure how this conversation was going to go down, and with my brief but shady history with Pete, I wasn't going to take any chances. I had no secrets anymore. None at all. To say my brief affair with Peter Broadus was the biggest mistake of my life was an understatement. He'd worked me hard for a while, telling me that Joshua had been cheating, and like an idiot, I fell for it. Hook, line, and sinker.

Revenge sex was the worst kind of sex. And there hadn't even been anything going on with Joshua. But we were past all that now. Joshua and I were good. We never talked about Pete and were both glad that he was no longer a part of our group. Very glad.

"What is it, Peter? We're kind of busy here."

"Oh, sorry. I was hoping to speak to Midas. Is he around?" he asked, sounding slightly irritated at my unwillingness to have a conversation with him.

"He's not here, Pete. It's just me and Joshua. Whatever you need to say to Midas, you can say to us."

"It's kind of private. He's not answering his cell phone. Are you sure he's not around?" Pete asked with his usual attitude.

"I'm sure. For the record, you didn't just abandon Midas on Crenshaw Road, you know. You abandoned all of us, Peter. We all deserve an apology if that's why you're calling. What the hell were you thinking? You know what, it doesn't even matter. What do you want? Whatever you have to say, I'm sure none of us are interested in hearing it."

After a long pause, he said in a ragged voice, "I wasn't thinking that day, Sierra. I let fear take over. I can't say I'm sorry enough. To both of you. I know you don't want to hear that—you either, Joshua. I know you're both listening, and I am completely sorry. If I could talk to you guys, you know, face to face, I think I could explain."

I was at a genuine loss here. Joshua shrugged, opened the office door and walked out, clearly disgusted with hearing

Pete's voice. They'd come to a kind of peace when Peter was working with us, but I knew they'd never actually be friends. I couldn't blame him. Typical of Pete to want to pretend he'd done nothing wrong. How was I supposed to interpret that? I picked up the receiver. There were so many reasons to be angry at Peter; I just couldn't pick one. But something inside of me, call it my weak spot, kind of felt sorry for him. I'd known the guy for too long to completely give up on him. Joshua wouldn't agree with me on that, and Midas was certainly done with Pete.

D. O. N. E.

But I needed to hear him out. Whether anyone else wanted to or not.

"I'm sorry about Jocelyn," he said. "I'm sorry about her most of all. I should have been with you guys. I loved her, Sierra. As best as I could. I'm not great at loving people. As you know."

"I'm not interested in hearing about your love life, Peter Broadus. And if you haven't completely pickled your brain, you'll keep off that subject when you do speak to Midas. It was his girlfriend you hooked up with, remember?"

"Me and Sara, it wasn't what you think, Sierra."

"What is that supposed to mean?"

He sighed and said, "I remember everything. I wish I could forget—that we could all forget. Please, let Midas know that I called and that I need to talk with him." *Ah, there we have it. It's all about Peter and his needs.* "I'm better, Sierra. I've been clean for three months. I'm back in Mobile, and I plan to stay. Please, just tell him?" he pleaded.

With a tap of my pen, I agreed and hung up the phone. I made a note for Midas and put it on his desk. I wasn't going to advise him one way or another. If he allowed Peter back into his life, that was up to him, but no way was Pete going to have another opportunity to leave me in the backwoods of Mississippi.

Fifteen minutes later, we were loaded up and ready to roll to Brady Hall. It was a close case, only four blocks from the Gulf Coast Paranormal office. I liked that. Going out of town for a case couldn't be avoided at times, but knowing I could go home to Emily, Bozo and Sherman was the best feeling in the world. Which reminded me, I needed to pick up dog food in the morning. Those guys were eating me out of house and home. At least the dogs were friends now. Jocelyn's big floppy white dog loved Emily, but he and Bozo had a few run-ins at the beginning of his stay with us. Now that everyone had their own toys and blankets and supper dishes, things were great. Mostly.

After a few trips to the van to collect our equipment, we settled in and I led the team around the property. Bonita decided not to come; she gave me the keys earlier. Helen was in one of her rare loving moods and ended our conversation with a hug. I told her what Bonita had said about us getting rid of the "ghost" that was haunting Brady Hall, but Helen assured me she had made no such promise.

"She's genuinely upset. Really upset. She's desperate for answers."

I genuinely liked Helen. She was strikingly beautiful and eloquent in speech, if sometimes a bit standoffish. She had a wonderful vocabulary, but there were times she came off as if she were speaking down to you. She was a bit moody but personable. I was relieved that she and Bruce were on this investigation with us because Joshua and I wouldn't be enough to cover this property effectively. It wasn't as large as the Crescent Theater, but it was nonetheless larger than a home. Here recently, we hadn't had too many residential cases. Mostly we were called to landmarks or commercial construction sites.

After our walk-through together, we began setting up cameras. We'd only gotten to the second camera when there was a knock on the front door. Joshua peeked out the window curiously and whispered, "It's a guy."

I rolled my eyes. *Well, duh. I didn't expect it to be a ghost. But then again....*

"Can you see what he wants?" And with that, he went back to working on his cord issue. I dutifully accepted my role as our spokesperson. I walked to the door but only opened it a crack.

"Hi. May I help you?"

"Hi. I am looking for Bonita Hutchinson. I'm here for the open house. That's tonight, isn't it?" The man unfolded the brochure he had in his hand.

Oh, shoot. Were these kinds of interruptions going to happen all night?

"I am so sorry about that. The open house had to be postponed for a few days. We're working on it, I mean, taking care of a few things first. We want the place to be perfect. Maybe you should call Mrs. Hutchinson and ask her about rescheduling. Is her number on that brochure?" I smiled as I slipped outside and attempted to close the door behind me. I wasn't quick enough because a red beam of light hit the stranger on the shoulder, and he glanced up to identify the source of the light.

"Is that a laser? What's going on in there? Hold on a second. I thought I recognized your face. You're what's her name...the ghost hunter. Sierra, right? Are you investigating Brady Hall?" He laughed a little and I shrugged, unsure what to say. It had always been our policy to keep investigations under wraps and not share them with the public at large, and here was this guy catching us red-handed setting up cameras.

"My name is Sierra, but I can't give you much more information than that. I can tell Bonita that you came by. What is your name, sir?"

"I get it. Mum's the word. My name is Evan Madison. I'm an investigator too. I had no idea that this place might be haunted, and just for the record, that doesn't turn me off as a buyer. In fact, I kind of like the idea of a place having a back story. You can't give me any clues at all, Sierra?" Evan swung his bangs to the side. He wore his hair kind of long; at least his bangs were long, as if he'd just stepped out of the 1990s.

"No, I can't, but I will tell Bonita that you came by. Have a nice evening, Evan," I said as he went back down the steps and hurried down the sidewalk. As I walked back into the house, I looked to see what kind of vehicle he was driving. A green luxury sedan, maybe a Benz? It was an antique, that was for sure. That's all we needed. Some rich fanboy hanging out mucking up the investigation. So much for anonymity.

I headed back inside and explained to the team what was up. "Let's make sure we have all of the blinds closed and...hey, who is that?" I pointed to the end of the hallway.

Everyone's attention turned to the empty doorway where I was staring. I could've sworn I saw someone there for the briefest of seconds. Was it possible that Evan Madison had come with a friend? Did his friend slip inside, or was I seeing something else?

"Did anyone else see that?" Everyone silently stared down the dark hallway.

Bruce spoke first. "I haven't seen anything. What did it look like?"

"About five feet. Dark. No facial features, arms or legs. It sailed from right to left. It didn't make any noise, just kind of slid. Really fast." I laughed at my own description. Man, I really had seen something. I know I did. Was it a trick of the light? Or something else?

Bruce and Joshua were immediately headed down the hallway. There were no openings to come in or out of. No open doors or windows. Nothing that could have allowed for light or shadow to move around in such a way as to project a human figure. After another few minutes of posing Helen in the hallway and trying to recreate the image, I called it.

"Let's chalk that up to personal experience and hope we caught it on camera."

We set up our monitoring station in the kitchen because it was relatively quiet and out of the way. As far as we knew, there wasn't any activity happening in the kitchen. "I guess we should start work by focusing on the mirror and the carpet where Bonita had her accident."

"I'll keep an eye on the cameras," Helen offered. That was slightly different than the original plan, but I didn't argue with her.

"Okay. So, let's do this," I said. Joshua turned the lights out in the kitchen as we headed out. It was the last light on in the house. The place was hidden in complete darkness, and the feelings that I got yesterday of the strange yet elusive presence were completely gone. It was as if I had imagined the whole thing. Even when we were up on the second floor running a cord to that camera earlier, it felt eerily quiet. Like whatever had been there had actually left the building. Could this thing be moving up and down the block? There was no backyard here, but there were buildings on either side. Both of them were vacant, so that was definitely a possibility. Entities, energies and ghosts all liked empty spaces. Mostly, they wanted to be left alone, but if you came into their space and they were strong enough, they would let you know about it. If that was the case, if this thing was moving, capturing evidence could prove to be a challenge. But I'd seen that shadow. That I had seen with my own two eyes, and I hadn't felt a thing!

"We'll have to turn the lamp on if we want to replicate the original lighting situation," Joshua suggested.

"Right, Joshua. Britney said the only light on was the lamp over there. So, let's try to recreate the illusion, or whatever this was, by turning that light on and leaving everything else off. She might be mistaken, though. If we aren't successful with the lamp, let's try to debunk it with the overhead light." I shivered as if a rabbit ran over my grave.

"From the angle of the picture, I think she stood over there. Britney was not in the picture, and the face was kind of at an angle. Would you guys agree?" Joshua asked as he moved gingerly across the room, avoiding the carpet. I should've never told those guys that Bonita had an accident on the rug. Clearly, she had it cleaned. My husband was so weird about that sort of thing. You would think after having a daughter, he would be less squeamish about bodily fluids, but that wasn't true at all.

"Why don't you snap a few pictures with your phone, Sierra? That's what she was using, an iPhone, right? I'll stand by the window. If it was a true reflection, that is about where the person would have been standing. Bruce, why don't you use your camera too?"

We snapped and reviewed, snapped and reviewed but couldn't recreate the image. No matter what kind of lighting, the angle was off and Joshua's face wasn't anything but handsome. Not skeletal at all. I sometimes forget how attractive he was and how much I loved him. Yeah, I forgot that a lot.

I wasn't giving up on this yet. "Let's try something else. Why don't you stand on the porch, Joshua, and I will take a few more shots? Maybe Britney wasn't completely honest, or she didn't notice there was someone pranking her. Maybe there was someone standing outside on the porch. If the curtains were open, then it's certainly possible."

"They'd have to be standing on the porch wearing a skeleton mask because I can't imagine how else you would recreate that face," Bruce said, unconvinced by my proposal. "That's no trick of the light. I think we're seeing a genuine apparition."

"Anything is possible. You guys know that," I said with a faint, friendly smile. "But let's give it a try anyway. Then maybe we should tackle some EVPs. You know, on second thought, why don't you take the pictures with my phone and I'll stand on the porch? I think the person in the picture is a little taller than me, but we'll see how this works. You'd be too tall."

"Roger that," Joshua said as he took my place and Bruce stood poised beside him with his expensive camera. Stepping out onto the porch, I glanced around hoping I wouldn't spot Evan Madison again. Nope. He was gone. I posed on the porch, but it was difficult to see inside. These windows needed a good cleaning, I thought as I hovered around the edge of the porch. I moved around in different positions as Josh took pictures.

I stepped back inside and again felt an odd chill. I closed and locked the door behind me, eager to see how those photos turned out. "Any luck? Do I look like an angry skeleton?"

"Uh, not a skeleton, but this is weird. Hold on a second; you take a look for yourself."

"What? Did we catch an image?" I asked curiously as he handed me the phone. "You're freaking me out, Joshua McBride." Bruce was peering into his camera, but he wasn't sharing either.

I tapped on the phone screen to blow up the image.

I wasn't there.

Chapter Seven—Sierra

"That's not something you see every day. How can we account for the absence of my image? That's not possible, as far as I know. You should see me or some part of me. My head, my arm. At least a shadow or something, right?" I stared at the strange photo. Just thinking about this made me sick. Yeah, that was true. Sick and queasy. I did not wish to make a big deal out of it, but this strange photo bothered me. This activity felt personal.

"Why don't you try it, Joshua? You step out on the porch and let me take your picture."

"Sure," he agreed sunnily as he exchanged places with me. Bruce and I took pictures of the porch without Joshua and then with my husband posing at and then near the window. It only took a few seconds to discover that the phenomenon was completely isolated to my reflection. We couldn't replicate it, even when Bruce gave it a shot.

"This is crazy. Do you think someone or something could be manipulating the photograph? Is this possible? Maybe I should go back out there. But then again..." I shivered. "This is giving me the creeps, y'all."

Bruce's bushy eyebrows lifted dramatically. "Perhaps we should stick to the original task—debunking the apparition. I had a chance to read your write-up, and Bonita Hutchinson's report is slightly different from Britney's. In Bonita's report, the woman in the mirror was on the opposite side...that would be the left side. This entity, if that's the title we're going with, can move. It's not stationary. It's probably not residual."

"Which begs the question, where did this mirror come from? Is it original to Brady Hall? And not to be an asshole, but do you think these ladies are trying to pull a fast one here?" Joshua examined the mirror with a flashlight. "I don't want to believe that, but it is very possible. We've seen firsthand here today that not everyone is turned off if they think a property might be haunted. That could actually be a selling point."

I rolled my eyes at that idea. "Not a chance. Bonita wants to sell this house, and I don't think she'd lie about it. She was terrified. Really terrified, Joshua. She confessed to urinating on herself. That's not something you do unless it really happened. Let's do some EMF readings around the mirror and in this room and maybe try some EVP work. Bruce, will you catch that light, please?"

The three of us went into dark mode and got to work. The EMF didn't register much of anything, and we spent a good hour in the dark moving around in different locations. We took turns sitting in the chair, on the sofa and even on the floor. Our initial reviews of the audio recording provided nothing. No clues at all. There was a possibility that a later review of the audio would reveal evidence, but at the moment, we had nothing to go on. I was beginning to wonder if maybe this thing had vacated the building. There were plenty of placcs to go. Supposedly, this room was the hotspot for the activity, but so far, we were striking out except for my odd photos. I was all for trying that again. I needed to try it again; just to be sure it wasn't coming after me. That happened sometimes. Negative spirits loved harassing the living that saw them. Often just for funsies, but it was never fun when you were the focus of a paranormal attack.

As the three of us pondered our next step, Helen's voice came over the walkie-talkie. She wasn't that far away; the kitchen was just two rooms over, and the sound of her voice in my ear and on the microphone gave it an odd stereo effect.

"I think you guys should come see this. We have activity on the second floor."

I followed Bruce and Joshua back to the kitchen. When we stepped into the kitchen, I could see Helen's face just a few inches from the monitor. She was staring hard at whatever it was she'd spotted. "Good eye, Helen. What do you have?"

"Temperature fluctuations. Multiple temperature fluctuations. They came out of the rooms and converged in the hallway and then disappeared. It was unnerving. I know we recorded it all, but I'm not sure how to loop it back. Joshua, can you do the looping thing? It happened really quickly and only lasts a few seconds, but it was definitely multiple targets."

"Sure, no problem." Joshua leaned over her and clicked the mouse, and the video began to play. One second the hallway was empty, and the next there were multiple blobs of color. And then it was empty again. It reminded me of a weatherman's radar when pop-up summer storms appeared. Suddenly red, suddenly green, suddenly gone. And Helen was right, all the anomalies had gathered in the hallway and then sailed off-camera where we couldn't see them, seemingly toward the staircase. I left the others alone as I traveled to the bottom of the stairs with a flashlight in hand. Nothing at all. I took a few steps up the staircase, but that queasy feeling hit me again.

Yuck. Okay, whatever you are, back the hell up.

I left the staircase and went back to the kitchen. "See anything?" Joshua asked hopefully.

"Nope. Let's see it again, please." I watched the footage again and again. It was bizarre. It was as if one minute there was nobody there, and the next three—no, make that four—anomalies invaded the space and quickly vanished.

Bruce said in an excited voice, "Would you mind playing that again? Maybe slow it down a bit more?"

"Here, you take the com, Joshua." Helen slid out of the chair, and Josh slid into it. Within a few seconds, my husband had pulled up the clip again and was playing it at a super-slow speed. It was Helen who began deciphering shapes first. She picked up her pencil and pointed at the screen. "That looks like a man's head and shoulders. See how it takes shape before it leaves the screen? It's as if they were formulating as they hit the staircase. I count four entities. It is clearly something with strange heat patterns. Not a living person, and it can't be bugs or drafts. Everything is locked down here. We checked all that. I am sure of it." Helen's rare excitement surprised me, but she was right. It couldn't be anything else except what we believed it was—ghosts!

Bruce suggested we continue on. "Let's strike while the iron is hot! Helen, let's head upstairs and take a look around. We should probably start on the staircase since that's where we assume they went. Now would be the time to try some EVPs too, I think."

"I'm going too," Joshua announced as he reached for the SLS. He smiled at me as I frowned.

Shoot. Odd man out. Again. This must be how Midas feels on these investigations when we all volunteer to go into the dark, spooky rooms. We are a bunch of crazy people.

"I'll keep an eye on you guys. Get up there!" I surrendered to their excitement. Honestly, I wanted to race up those steps myself, but as I reminded everyone all the time, Gulf Coast Paranormal was a team. I couldn't take over every aspect of the investigation. Even though I was truly Miss Bossy Pants. Joshua nailed me with that nickname on our first date.

As soon as they stepped out of the room, I followed their movements on the monitors. Bruce was leading the way with his night vision camera. Helen was right behind him holding her digital recorder and an EMF detector, while Joshua brought up the rear with the SLS. I tapped on the keyboard so I could see firsthand exactly what it was Joshua was seeing. If anything. I reminded myself to be quiet, but the tension was so thick that you could cut it with a knife. I reached for my walkie-talkie but thought better of it. Those guys knew what they were doing. They didn't need me to armchair coach them. The trio of investigators paused on the stairs.

"Starting the EVP session now. Joshua, Helen and Bruce on the staircase of Brady Hall right after witnessing those anomalies on the screen. Hi. My name is Helen, and these are my friends Joshua and Bruce. We are not here to bother anyone. We certainly don't want to scare you, but Bonita invited us to come and talk to you. You may not know this, but you scared her in the downstairs mirror. And you scared Britney too."

In this case, I was pretty certain this entity knew what it was doing.

Not a sound was detected. Helen kept going. "Are you trying to scare people? Are you there? Make a sound so I know that you can hear me. Can you knock on a wall?" Helen stayed in place as Bruce moved ahead to the upstairs hallway with his infrared. Josh remained standing in one position near the stairs. Nothing was mapping on his SLS. Not a dang thing. But the lurching in my stomach told me that we were onto something.

Something was about to happen.

Remember to breathe, Sierra Kay. They are more afraid of you than you are of them.

"Right, sure," I whispered to myself as I took a few even breaths. I can't say why, but I kept glancing at the kitchen doorway. Were my eyes playing tricks on me again? Were the shadows actually moving? I swear I'd seen a person-sized shadow moving earlier. Moving and shifting.

Helen kept going like a true trouper. "I was downstairs a few minutes ago, and I saw you moving around up here. All of you. Are you friends? Is this your family? What are you doing up here? Can you tell me your name? We don't want to hurt you. We really want to help." Helen was in the hallway now, standing approximately where the largest anomaly had been spotted earlier. She paused and tapped Bruce's shoulder as she stared straight ahead. From my vantage point, I couldn't see very much, but I strained to try and see something.

Anything.

"Did you guys see that? A tiny white light zipped from that door to that door." I hadn't caught it, but that didn't mean Helen didn't see it. It was hard to capture orbs and lights on the camera. Capturing real evidence was a game of chance.

"Keep going, Helen," I heard Bruce encourage her as he put his camera down and stared into the darkness. Sometimes your eyes were the best tools to use, but we needed evidence. The senses were powerful if we paid attention to them. Human beings came equipped with danger sensors. Most people ignored them. Until it was too late.

"What do you want? Are you stuck here? Are you the same person who Bonita and Britney saw in the mirror? Do you need help?" I briefly caught a blip on Joshua's display, but it was gone as fast as I could blink. Not enough footage to capture or record and study.

I reached for the walkie-talkie to offer some suggestions when a loud crashing sound from the front room startled me. Had the mirror fallen off the wall? I was on my feet, my hand over my heart in shock. I expected my fellow investigators to come barreling down the steps, and when they didn't I tapped on the radio. I took a few hesitant steps toward the doorway that led to the parlor, but my feet did not want to make that trip. The queasiness returned, and I detected a sour smell.

No, not sour. Rotten. It smelled rotten. Like decomposition.

Oh hell.

"Joshua? Did you hear that? Where are you?"

"Hear what?"

I took a deep breath and walked toward the parlor. There was no time to wait.

Chapter Eight—Cassidy

Midas had kindly offered to pick up dinner. I wasn't up to hanging out in a restaurant tonight, even though the scenery in Gulf Shores was completely amazing. There was something so refreshing about being close to the ocean. I didn't plan beach trips nearly enough. I took a morning run along the shore before the festival and found it completely invigorating. I wasn't exactly running on all six cylinders yet—that surgery had taken it out of me—but I made slow progress. No marathons for a while, but in a few months, I'd definitely be competing again.

Midas supported me in my physical fitness journey, but recently I got the feeling that he'd be just as happy if I gave up sketching, painting and drawing altogether. Paranormally speaking. He didn't seem to understand that I didn't really have a choice in the matter. Especially now, after twenty-five plus investigations. My work with Gulf Coast Paranormal had left me extremely open to the Other Side, probably too open if Midas was to be believed. I loved that he cared about me, but I didn't like the feeling that he thought I couldn't handle myself. Granted, I should have stepped back on the Oakleigh case, but other than that, I'd been just fine. Mostly.

Which brought me back to the moment. I only had a little while before Midas returned with our chow. I tossed around the idea of showing him my sketch but voted that down. Not just yet. We'd had such a great time here at the Gulf Shores Art Festival that I didn't want to dampen his mood. And it had been so romantic. I hated for that to end because he was so happy, but the Other Side was reaching out to me. I suspected that the team was working on a case; Midas was the worst at trying to be covert with a phone call.

Another reason to love him.

The investigation could be the reason why these images were showing up in my mind. It didn't normally happen unless we were working to help a client. Why wouldn't he tell me about it? I couldn't say, but eventually, we'd have to talk about this. I took my small sketchbook out of my backpack and opened it to my work in progress. This face, as normal as it looked, was the face of a killer.

A crazy person. Why did they always have to be crazy?

A murderess. She hadn't just been fantasizing about killing her lover, she'd done it. I could feel her gleefulness. She was so happy that she'd done what she'd set out to do. Oh, and so much more. So much more.

Over the past year—no, make that two years—I'd learned to follow my intuition with my art. By doing so, I had come into contact with a variety of dead. In some cases, not dead but missing. Oh, but some of them had been nothing short of crazy. Like the woman from the Crescent Theater—Estella Winters had been her name. Why was I thinking about her? I shook my head at the memory of that case.

I put the sketchbook on the small dining table and turned the light on. I snapped a picture of this mystery woman and sent it to Sierra along with a message.

Whatever you're doing, be careful. She's watching you, Sierra.

Even as I typed, I knew it was true. Absolutely true. Sierra faced danger, and maybe not just her. She didn't text me back immediately, but she eventually sent me a smiley face along with a thanks. My thumbs hovered over the keyboard. Should I ask her for details? Better not. I decided to give Midas a chance to tell me what was up. He needed to do that. I put my sketch away and answered a few emails and a phone call from a patron. It was incredible how many people loved my art. Not my paranormal artwork, nobody got to see those pieces but the team. They were too precious and personal. My patrons loved my stills and scenes of life. Tomorrow was the last day of the festival, and although I was glad I'd come, I would also be glad to get home.

I missed my cat, Domino, and my bed.

Midas sent me a text. He was on the way back but decided to make a pit stop, some sort of surprise for me. I couldn't imagine what that could be, but I was certainly curious. And also, very unsettled.

Very. Unsettled.

I took the sketchbook out of the bag and reached for my denim pencil bag. I didn't even care which one I grabbed. I had to start on this new sketch. This wouldn't be the same subject. This other girl—I didn't get her name, but I knew her face well—had deep-set eyes and thick eyebrows. By today's standards, she would be considered plain, but she believed herself to be quite beautiful. And the man she'd been involved with thought she was something quite special. At least for a little while. Even as he rejected her, he considered her quite the prize. But that was all she was...a prize.

Enough about her.

This other woman, slightly older than the first, was thinner with a narrow face. Her brown eyes were almond-shaped, only slightly tilted, like a wolf's, and her eyebrows were naturally thin. She had pallid skin, colorless and slightly greasy as if she'd not quite removed all her cold cream. Her eyes had that odd shine of brilliance. The kind of shine you see when someone has an idea that could change the world. Or burn it down.

Elizabeth. That was her name.

And she had a brilliant mind. Elizabeth was much more than people saw; she had a way with words and numbers. All these thoughts came to me as I sketched the lines of her brows, her slender jawline, and her ear. She did not like her ears very much, but it was the fashion to show your earlobes with an upswept bun.

Thank goodness Rebecca didn't have her ears. Rebecca had been a beautiful child. But nobody knew about Rebecca. Elizabeth's daughter remained her own treasure, her own secret. Nobody would ever know what had happened.

As I drew, a tear streamed down my face. Oh, the sadness. So sad. And not only about Rebecca. Sad over Elizabeth's husband, and her first husband and the other one and the life she'd lost.

Adeo, yes, that's his name. *A-day-oh*. He thought he knew her, but he never really did. He couldn't begin to grasp any of it.

My fingers began to shake. *No. I have to stop. Midas will be back soon! Midas will return, and I don't want him to catch me sketching. He will worry over it and discourage me, but I have to keep going.* I reached for a different pencil as I wiped the salty tears off my face.

This lady's sorrow ran deep. Far too deep for me, but I was entranced by her.

I had to know more about what the ghost wanted from Sierra. This woman didn't want me to know her secret, but I hummed away her worries.

No worries, no worries. Your secrets are safe with me.

Strangely enough, she seemed to trust me. She stepped aside and let me see.

This girl. She hates me. She holds me here. She is always stealing the spotlight. Can't you see her?

"Tell me more," I whispered to the ghost in my mind.

Oh, yes. Lynette. Yes, she's an upstart. Lynette always reaches for what is not hers. Can't you see that? Can you see what she has done? She took everything!

But you'll never have Adeo. Not in any true sense. And my Rebecca will always be mine...

Chapter Nine—Elizabeth

Clutching the wrinkled paper in my ink-stained fingers, I paced the carpet replaying the scene in my mind again and again. Adeo believed that *Ode to Rebecca* was perfect as it was, but I did not agree. There was nothing good about it without this scene. It lacked the depths of sorrow that I knew should be there.

"Wife, we cannot afford the additional set, not to mention the wardrobe required to fulfill such an endeavor. A water scene would be remarkably difficult to present to the audience." His posture stiffened, just as my resolve stiffened.

"Surely not, Adeo. We are artists, are we not? Anything is possible on the stage. I believe we can do this. We have always been a step ahead of the competition, and the Red Velvet Room is luring far too much of our audience away. We must make these changes, not only for me but for our future. People already love the play—we know that. But when they hear of this added scene, they will flock again to Brady Hall to see it for themselves! Printing the playbills costs nearly nothing, and it will take no time. This makes sense, artistically and financially. You must see that."

Adeo sat in his favorite cushioned chair. I had yet to win him over, but I was determined. How could I explain to him how important this was to me? I could not; I would not. But I saw this scene in my dream, and I knew it belonged here. It would explain everything! It wasn't me! I did not do this. How could I have committed such a crime? A crime against my own daughter? Surely, I would recall it if I had done it.

My dream provided the answer, and it had to be in the play. For Rebecca! It had to have been inspired by a Higher Power, one that wanted me to know the truth about the day I could not remember. When the world went red and, when I finally came to my senses, I found my daughter gone.

But what about the time before, Elizabeth. What about Little George?

"I do not wish to cast aspersions, dearest, but this changes the play completely. Many fans of *Ode to Rebecca*, including me, have always believed that Lucrezia killed her daughter. Am I wrong?"

My heart sank in my chest. *Oh, I have been too transparent. I have told you too much! Did the entire world believe that I was a killer?* No! They did not. Adeo had no idea that I had ever had a child, or that I had lost her so cruelly.

"Besides, Lynette is too far behind on her sewing already. If we were to add this scene, it would mean bringing on another seamstress. Perhaps two."

I fell to my knees and laid my head in his lap. I had won this battle; I could hear it in his words.

If we were to...

That always meant my wish would be granted. This meant that Adeo believed in my vision, believed in me. And in a strange way, I interpreted it to mean that he believed in my innocence.

No, Elizabeth! How can he believe that you are innocent? He knows nothing!

"Adeo," I whispered into his jacket. "Thank you." I was tempted to weep, but other emotions arose, ones I did not expect. I wanted Adeo, in the way a wife should want her husband. Yes, despite everything I knew, I wanted him still. Our couplings were not regular; I had a deep and abiding fear of pregnancy. Not again. I would never get pregnant again. But just this once. Only once, to ignite my muse and fulfill the longing of my heart and body. To give Adeo what he needed from me. How could I not love him, despite his shortcomings? How could I not love him, knowing my own sins? I could never hold his against him.

"Will you always love me, Adeo? Only me?" I tilted my face up to him and begged him to lie to me. I knew whatever he said would be a lie.

Adeo kissed me passionately. "Who else could I trust with my heart, my darling? Of course, only you ever, Elizabeth."

I took his promises of fidelity to heart but only for the moment. As all things were with Adeo. I sensed his body tense with desire beneath my touch. Strangely enough, as my passion rose, so did my jealousy. I felt great temptation to confront Adeo about his affections for Lynette Farris.

But I resisted.

Another time. I had this small victory now, and I would have this moment. As I helped Adeo slip out of his jacket, he asked in a husky voice, "Tell me, Elizabeth. How do you see the scene? Is there a part for me?"

I tossed his jacket on the chair behind him and kissed him into silence. He fumbled with the buttons of my dress, and I laughed with delight. "Always, Adeo. You are the star. Of course there is a part for you."

I heard the footsteps of one of the staff tiptoeing away. Would we make love right here in the parlor? I began leading Adeo from the open room as my body burned for him. I needed this moment. I must have this moment!

"What about Ronald and Lynette, dearest? Our understudies have been patiently waiting for some small part to play. Don't you think we should include them in this addition? I can tell you it would make Lynette very happy. I worry that she will leave us, and such a great talent she is, Elizabeth."

"Worry? Why should you worry over Lynette, Adeo?"

I savagely released his hand. How dare he try to coerce me into rewarding his latest conquest with a part in my play? How dare he ask me such a thing at this moment? It was beyond the pale! Adeo's expression revealed so much. He knew that I knew. He was an intelligent man, too intelligent to challenge me. I would never give Lynette more than what she already had. She would not have my husband!

"You dare ask me to make room for your lover? Even as we are about to make love?" I spit out angrily.

"Elizabeth! Do not say something you will regret. You are my wife. You are speaking like a little fool."

We said nothing but stared at one another. Who would flinch first? Of course, it would be me. I looked away to brush away an unexpected tear.

"Sweet Elizabeth. Let us behave as a married couple should. I love only you, only you ever, Elizabeth. It is the truth."

With shaking fingers, I began buttoning up my dress. I snorted at his pleas. "Before you accuse me of being mistaken or hysterical, let me reveal this to you, husband. I am not crazy. I know all about you and your sordid affairs in the closets and in the icehouse and wherever else you decide to make a conquest! Do you understand how you humiliate me? Each time you parade around with these women? I know all about the things that you've done with Lynette and so many others. I kept my silence because I believed that you loved me, Adeo. I believed that you cared about us. Despite your fleshly weaknesses, I believed you cared for me, but how wrong I have been! You care only about yourself!"

"No, Elizabeth. That is not true. I have loved only you. Ever!"

"You will end this affair, Adeo, or I will leave you. And I will take Rebecca—she's my daughter—and I will leave you!"

Adeo smiled, and it unsettled me. "You will take Rebecca? You mean the play, don't you?"

I stuttered my response. I could not tell him that. "The play, I mean the play! Do you think you have it all, Adeo? All my money? All my talent? Nothing could be further from the truth, my love. I am rich beyond your wildest imaginations." I smiled at my own statement. It made me more confident. "I have more of everything. You will never find it. Never in a million years. Let her go, or I will let you go," I snarled at him as I jutted out my chin to emphasize the seriousness of the matter.

Adeo's face was aflame with anger, but I had learned he would not challenge me when money was at stake. Never. And I was telling the truth. I did have much more, thanks to my first husband's generous estate. And the second's.

And my poor Rebecca's death.

Dangerous things happened when I became enraged. The image of Rebecca floating in the water face first, purple bruises around her neck, appeared in my mind, but I pushed them away. I would not allow my guilt to be a distraction. No, my own sins would not rule me when Adeo's sins were much worse.

But he wasn't backing down. He wasn't giving way. He snarled at me, and his mischievous smile grew wider by the second.

"Let me tell you then what I know, Elizabeth. Let me tell you what I know."

Adeo nudged me into the bedroom and closed the door behind him. His voice dropped to a lower octave, soft but careful. Measured. He tilted his head down, but his eyes were fastened on me.

"Let me tell you what I know..."

Chapter Ten—Sierra

By the time I determined the source of the foam beads I had found all over the house, my beanbag chair was utterly and completely destroyed. Neither Bozo nor Sherman wanted to confess to their crimes, but I had no doubt these two were the reason for the destruction.

"Bad boy, Sherman! Bad boy, Bozo! What did my beanbag chair ever do to you?"

Sherman whined intuitively while Bozo panted with his bead-covered tongue hanging out like nothing was wrong. "Thanks, guys. This is just what I needed today, a big old mess to clean up. It's not like you don't have toys and plenty of things to wreak havoc on. You're both going to go to time-out."

Sherman whimpered as I reached for his collar. I hated putting the furry kids in time-out, but they needed to understand that this was not acceptable behavior. Sometimes they just got carried away with their nonsense, and when that happened, things got destroyed. At least they were getting along. Chances were good that one of the two of them had laid claim to my beanbag chair and the other one wasn't having it. I could just imagine in my mind's eye the tug-of-war that occurred before my beanbag was torn apart.

I'd barely gotten the two dogs into their kennels when Emily decided to add to the ambiance of my day. She screamed as loudly as she could, which indicated it was lunchtime. My daughter had no idea how to cope with her hunger pangs.

"I'm on the way, Em," I called from the other room, pretending to be calm.

I'm calm. So calm. Breathe in. Breathe out.

On my way to retrieve the vacuum cleaner, I peeked in on my daughter, and she was just fine. Emily was sitting in her playpen with her finger in her mouth, screaming at the top of her lungs. Seeing me didn't relieve her unhappiness. And now Bozo was howling. "It must be nice to get up and leave the house in the morning, Joshua," I muttered to myself as I headed off to the broom closet to get the vacuum cleaner. Emily managed to reach a higher decibel level, and I reconsidered my plan of action.

Well, I guess cleaning all this up can wait until after I have Emily down for her nap.

About that time the doorbell rang, and now I wanted to cry. I let out a sigh as I walked to the front door, completely uncaring that this visitor was going to hear my daughter yelling at the top of her lungs.

Just keeping it real in the McBride household. Just keeping it real.

"Hey, Helen. What are you doing here?" I didn't mean that the way it sounded. It wasn't like I was unhappy to see her, but this was not great timing. I peeked around the corner to see if Bruce was with her, but she was alone. She was impeccably dressed and carrying an expensive purse. Man, she was always so put together. I was pretty sure I hadn't brushed my hair yet and had forgotten to refresh my deodorant when I woke up.

"As you can tell by the sound, it is feeding time at Casa McBride. Please, come on in and enjoy the fireworks." I slapped a big old smile on my face as I stepped out of the way. Helen politely stepped inside and stayed in the foyer for a few seconds. I could tell she wasn't used to hanging out with screaming children.

"If you don't mind, Helen, I have to feed Emily. Why don't you come into the kitchen? That's where the action is happening," I said and then laughed dryly. "What brings you by today?"

"I have some information about the investigation at Brady Hall. I guess I could've emailed it to you, but I wanted to...um...let me help you with that." And the "that" she was referring to was my daughter. I picked up Emily's wriggling behind and put her on my shoulder. But Emily wasn't willing to be consoled by anyone, much less a near stranger. It's food she wanted. No love. No attention. Food.

"No, it's fine. I've got her. She can be quite a handful. And loud, in case you missed that part." Helen trailed after me as I stepped into the kitchen. At least the kitchen was clean. Which was remarkable considering I had two dogs, a baby and Joshua. "Can I get you something? Some water or coffee? I think there's some coffee left in the pot."

"No, thank you, Sierra. I am fine. What can I do to help? I feel like I should do something."

"Be patient with us. Once I get her settled and manage to shove a few spoons of food in her mouth, she'll settle down. She's got a great vocal range, doesn't she?"

Helen smiled prettily. "It's been so long since I've been around a small child. It's not like riding a bicycle, you know. I don't think I could balance a child on my hip and navigate a kitchen at the same time, but you do it all so effortlessly. I truly admire you, Sierra. You are a rock star."

"Hardly. Unless rock stars own unruly pets and have diva daughters." I laughed again as I secured Emily in her high chair and pulled my chair close to hers.

Helen thought about my comment for a moment and then laughed. "You know, I've been watching quite a bit of reality television lately, and I think some of them do! Have you watched *Hip Hop Harlem*?"

"No, I can't say I have. Interesting title, though. And I can't believe you watch it." I snapped open the peaches and green beans and tied a bib around my daughter's chunky neck as she continued her squall-fest.

"I'm not as square as I look, Sierra."

"Square? Who says that?" I smiled as I wiped snot from my child's runny nose. Yep, she cried so much, her nose ran like an open hydrant.

"I bet she's going to grow up to be an amazing singer. She has quite a pair of lungs on her."

"You have no idea, Helen. I think she's amped up even more because her teeth are coming in. Can you imagine? My daughter is old enough to have teeth coming in! It blows my mind. How quickly time flies." It was a random comment but an honest appraisal of my life recently. And sure enough, like a magician pulling a rabbit out of a hat, my daughter magically quieted. I shook my head as she scarfed down her green beans.

"I swunny! Why would anyone get that excited about green beans?" Helen laughed as she dug in her bag. "She is really lovely, Sierra. Like a doll, just like you. Despite her red face and runny nose, she is a pretty little thing. Are you going to put her in preschool or daycare? I guess working with Midas, you have a little bit of an advantage. You could always take her to work with you. He's not a bad boss."

"Yes, that's true. But to be honest with you, work is like a little getaway for me. I probably shouldn't say that. I'm sure there will be some days that I cannot avoid bringing her with me, but I think getting her started early interacting with other children is the right way to go. I don't know. Joshua and I have been really lucky because my mother-in-law adores Emily. We haven't had to think about childcare much."

Silence passed between us as I fed my child. Then Helen said, "I am going to miss you all when I'm gone. I really have come to think of you all as a family. I know I'm not the easiest person to get along with, but I respect you, Sierra McBride. You are a good woman."

Why was this conversation making me tear up? I wiped at my eye while continuing to shovel food into Emily's open mouth. My daughter was a bottomless food pit.

"Thanks, Helen. That means a lot, and we're going to miss you too. *I'm* going to miss you. You guys are going to be hard to replace. Who knows, maybe we will investigate some areas in your new location. I mean—come on. Gettysburg? You're going to be so busy up there."

"I know. Bruce has lined us out for the next six months, but I am hoping to do something a little different. I like the occasional investigation, but I think I would like to try my hand at raising chickens. Try something peaceful and rural like that."

"You with chickens? I believe you could do that. So, no bed-and-breakfast?"

She shook her white head. "Those days are over, thank you. I want a small farm in the country, just big enough for the two of us and maybe a guest room. A place where we can spend our declining years in comfort."

"Declining years? Come on, Helen. You're far from declining," I said, laughing her statement off.

She chuckled, and we both got a kick out of that. "Thanks for saying so even though my body does not agree with you. But that's not why I came by. I wanted to share what I uncovered with you before the investigation tonight. I found bone-chilling details about the Brady Hall murder."

"It's true, then? There was an actual murder at Brady Hall?" I wiped at Emily's face halfheartedly with a clean kitchen towel as she resisted my efforts to do the job.

"Absolutely true. The Monterros were the couple involved. They owned the place and kept the original name, Brady Hall. Adeo Monterro was a bit of a playboy, but he was supposedly an intelligent businessman and for a while ran a successful playhouse and production company right from that location. He's the man who was murdered."

"Okay, I'm curious. What happened?"

Helen opened her file and read, "Adeo's wife, Elizabeth Monterro, was the suspect. However, after doing a bit of research, the local police discovered that there was no Elizabeth Blake Monterro. They could not track down anything about this woman or who she claimed to be. She was a true mystery woman, and Elizabeth refused to tell the police anything beyond what they already knew. She claimed she was born in Fort Lauderdale, Florida, but they checked with the authorities there. There had been no Blake family living in Fort Lauderdale at that time. But she was filthy rich. It was widely believed that it was her fortune that funded Adeo's vision. She was the money *and* the talent; he was the brains behind it all. He was a decent actor in his own right, but she was supposedly brilliant. People described him as handsome, affable and charismatic and were quite shocked at his murder."

I snorted. "Describes every playboy I have ever known. Was Elizabeth prosecuted for the murder? Do you think that's who is haunting the place?"

"Sadly enough, Elizabeth caught pneumonia in prison and died before her trial. Justice was never served for Adeo Monterro. And if she was innocent, as she claimed with her dying breath, there was no justice for her either."

A creepy feeling shimmied over my body, and Emily shuddered too. *Wow. That's weird. Please, God. My child is too little to be dealing with such abilities.* I swallowed as I gave her another bite. Her trusting eyes were clamped on mine, and I whispered to her, "It's okay, baby. Eat your food."

"I heard back from Bonita, and that mirror is original to the house. Could it be that Elizabeth is trying to make contact through that mirror?"

"Anything is possible—as you well know. But I don't know, Helen. Something feels off. It just feels like we're missing something."

"Well, this might interest you. Mrs. Monterro claimed that the prop knife had been replaced. But the police didn't believe her. They found it strange that she'd written this murder scene just a few weeks before and that she wrote the scene for herself and her husband. The detectives postulated that Mrs. Monterro planned this murder right from the beginning. Since Adeo was such a playboy, it wasn't hard for them to jump to their conclusions. Mrs. Monterro wanted to kill him because she was a jealous and scorned wife, and she wanted an audience to witness her wrath."

I whistled at that dramatic potential plot twist. I reached for the peaches and popped the cap as I listened to Helen's information. She was a proverbial well of historic fact when it came to Mobile's sordid history. Digging historical bones had been incredibly difficult on this case because I couldn't find much about Brady Hall. Apparently, though, Helen had mad research skills and hit the motherlode.

"So, if Elizabeth Monterro was telling the truth, then that means somebody else had to have set her up? Is that what you are thinking happened?"

"That is what I'm thinking. I think there is a murderer out there still. An injustice remains, and it needs to be corrected."

Emily nodded off now that her appetite settled down. I considered Helen's theory and whispered, "Let's keep all this in mind tonight and see if we can tempt Elizabeth to speak to us. Maybe she will be willing to tell us who actually killed her husband, or maybe she will confess. Either way, I am happy you came across this information. Thank you so much, Helen. Now, how about some peaches?" I showed her my peach-covered hands.

She wrinkled her nose at that suggestion. "Hard pass. I'm meeting my sweetheart for lunch at Mama's. I like my peaches as a cobbler." She put her papers back in her file and slid those into her purse. "But I'll see you tonight, Sierra. Please, don't get up. I'll show myself out."

I smiled my thanks. "Thank you for coming, and thanks for visiting me. I enjoyed this. Really. I sometimes forget what it's like to be in the adult world without dogs and screaming children."

Helen rose from the table and paused in the doorway. Her elegantly painted fingernails looked so bright compared to the white molding. If I had to name that color, I would call it Candy Apple Red.

Ugh, I am badly in need of a manicure.

"Don't be in a hurry to put these years behind you. Life is incredibly fleeting," she said softly. "See you tonight, Sierra." And with that, she left.

I smiled and lifted my sleeping daughter from her chair. I watched from the window as Helen drove away. With foam beads everywhere and clothing covered in peaches and green beans, I suddenly felt very blessed.

Life was too precious to wish it away.

Chapter Eleven—Sierra

About thirty minutes before Joshua and I were to head out to the Gulf Coast Paranormal offices, I got a Messenger notice from Rose, Midas' friend. I did a little digging earlier, just to be nosy. Rose had an interesting social media profile, to say the least. The woman was into all sorts of cool things like graveyard etchings and Day of the Dead makeup artistry, and she was a photographer. Her profile was littered with interesting grave markers, cemetery statues, sugar skulls, but nothing with her face.

Strangely enough, or maybe not so strangely, without looking at her face, Rose reminded me of the late Jocelyn Graves.

Got a minute?

Just a few. Leaving for investigation in 30.

Only take a sec.

Anytime you're ready.

Joshua went ahead so he could take Emily by Mrs. McBride's. The dogs were settled down, and the house was quiet. Quieter than it had been all day. I tapped on the laptop screen, anxious to meet this Rose character. No, not anxious. I was nervous, though I was not quite sure why. The screen flickered and then beeped to let me know we were connected.

"Hey, nice to meet you, Rose," I said awkwardly. "I'm Sierra." *Well, that was a pretty dopey intro. Who do you think she was expecting, dumbass?* My tired brain warned me that this would be a long night. I sipped my coffee as I tried to get it together. Man, I was so very tired.

"Yeah, you too. Midas calls you Little Sister, but he's not your brother, right?" she asked pointedly.

Um, ok. I wasn't sure where she was going with this line of questioning, so I just replied, "No, he's not. We're really close, though, like sister and brother. I couldn't tell you how that got started."

Actually, yes, I did. Sara nicknamed us that early on, but I didn't want to give Rose an opportunity to bring her up in any conversation. "Did you get a chance to look at those pictures I sent? What do you think? Are they legit?"

"They're unusual. That's for sure, man," Rose replied as she stared at the screen. Clearly, she was looking at the pictures even as we were speaking.

To make the silence less uncomfortable, I rambled on, "I'll be honest, I am not great at identifying phonies. It's not hard to pull a fast one on me when it comes to photos, so I am grateful for your help. Our client is in a desperate situation. The guy we used to work with a while ago, Peter Broadus, he was a whiz at this sort of thing. As you know, Jocelyn was too, but anyway...I'm rambling. What did you find out?"

Geez, Sierra, way to keep it together.

Rose tilted her head and studied me as if she wanted to say something, but she didn't. She was shockingly pretty, with piercing green eyes. *Oh yeah, there was more to this chick than meets the eye.*

She shook her head and got to business. "Well...I opened the photo in my Pandora's Box software. I don't know if you're familiar with PB, but it's a really awesome tool that helps you pick up patterns. Pictures are like fingerprints," she explained. "They have expected lines and clusters of pixels and all sorts of tells that identify them as originals."

"Neat," I said hurriedly. I hated being the last one to arrive at the office. Not a good look for the Boss Lady. I hoped she'd get to the point soon. She didn't.

"Pictures that have been manipulated in some way lack those original fingerprints. I don't find any evidence to show that this picture has been doctored in any way. It's a real image. An original. That doesn't mean that there wasn't someone standing around pretending to be a ghost, but there is definitely no bs going on as far as the actual picture." Rose paused and clicked on her screen. "Now, the picture you sent me last night...that one was really wack. That looks as if someone erased you. I mean, there's nothing to indicate that anyone is standing outside that window. But you say you were there, so I believe you. If the fingerprint grain is any indication, it seems as if an energy source blotted out your image. It takes a lot of energy to shield a solid object, Sierra. But according to the picture itself, you were not there. Period."

Rose's words tugged at my heart. What could this mean? Were the entities at Brady Hall telling me to stay away? Was I crossing some sort of line? Were they threatening to erase me if I came back? I got the feeling that I *was* being threatened, but I didn't know how to process that. I was definitely feeling unusually anxious.

"You sure you're cool? You seem worried," Rose said as she sipped her iced coffee, clearly unfazed by our exchange.

Midas had said not to bother trying to hide my feelings from her. He said she was *intuitive*, and dang it if it wasn't true. "Intimidating" was the word that came to my mind. Not sure why, since she seemed nice enough. She had icy white hair and perfect cat-eye makeup. She was pretty in an unassuming way, like she didn't know it and didn't care about it. It was obvious that she wasn't the kind to try to impress anyone. I was envious of her long lashes and dark painted nails, and vaguely recalled a day when I had the time and patience to try a new look.

Man, that's what I need. A day at the spa. Or two, or three.

"You know that ghosts can be a-holes. If it's targeting you, Sierra, it feels threatened." Even behind her glasses, her intense green eyes seemed to pierce right through me as she said, "You have abilities, don't you? Does anyone else on your team have abilities?"

"I do. Cassidy does, but she's not on this particular investigation. She's currently out of town."

"My advice, and you can take it or not, is to take a few minutes before you start the next stage of your investigation. Have a quiet conversation with whoever is in that house. Explain to them that you are there to help, not harm. They may not know the difference."

How odd that she would use the word "stage." "Uh, okay. Anything else?"

She smiled, showing perfect white teeth. "No. That's it. Message me if you need anything else. And Sierra, remember to breathe."

"Rose? I'm sorry to hear about Ben."

"Thanks. Later, Sierra." She smiled faintly, and just like that, Rose with the pretty green eyes and silver hair was gone.

I let out the breath I hadn't realized I was holding. I instantly remembered what Rose said.

Explain to them you are there to help...

Dang, that made so much sense.

I left the conversation feeling hopeful. I closed my laptop, grabbed my purse and keys, and headed to the office to catch the van. I intended to do exactly what Rose suggested, by myself and before anyone else got inside Brady Hall. Maybe there was a simple misunderstanding here. That was entirely possible.

We carried the same equipment as we did the night before. There was no change in tactics either, but we were all very quiet on the trip over. Helen had given us all a lot to think about. Her info was about all we did have, that and some interesting photographs that we captured last night. Plus that ghost light upstairs and a few odd reflections in the mirror. Okay, so we had quite a bit. But no apparitions, and no one was talking in any of the EVPs.

We were low on the evidence so far, to say the least. Unfortunately, that shadow figure I caught out of the corner of my eye had not been snapped with the camera, but we knew there was something going on. I talked to the team a little bit about what Rose said about the photos being untouched. That amazed everyone. I didn't go into detail about what she said about my image in that photo...or the absence of my image, to be exact.

Midas did not call to check in on us, and I completely forgot to call him. I guess everything was hunky-dory with him and Cassidy. I didn't like the fact that they were texting and calling me independently of one another, but that was a fight for another day. I just didn't have the energy for it.

"Guys, if you wouldn't mind giving me a minute in the house alone, I'd like to talk to whoever is there and just let them know that we don't intend any harm. There might be some confusion about why we are here. Rose suggested it, and I think it's a good idea."

"Do you think that's safe, going by yourself?" Joshua asked as he turned off the van. We were sitting in front of the house like a load of criminals. This would all be amusing if it wasn't so serious. Hopefully, nobody called the cops on us. This was a nice neighborhood, after all.

Joshua put his hand on my shoulder and squeezed it lovingly. "I mean, if there really is a murderer lingering around in the afterlife at Brady Hall, it might not want to talk. Whoever it is probably knows the jig is up. I don't want you taking more risks than you need to, Sierra Kay."

Why did he always say this? I couldn't help but roll my eyes at him.

"Yeah, me either. And quite frankly, I am tired, but I have to do this. If it doesn't make any change and doesn't affect anything, then no harm, no foul. It's hardly likely that I'll make things worse, but I'd like to cover my bases. Agreed, everyone? It should only take a few minutes."

Bruce tapped the back of the van seat. "Great idea. That will give us a few minutes to get everything together, and then we'll meet you inside."

I grabbed the keys to Brady Hall and went into the building with my "feelers" on. It was all quiet again. And in my mind's eye, I visualized multiple shadows creeping up the stairs and into the attic. These weren't shadow people. They weren't dark entities. They were ghosts. Dead people, and several of them. I wasn't going to chase them. That would certainly send the wrong message. Rose was right. They were afraid. All of them. I wondered why....

I went inside, stood on the stairs about midway up and called out politely, "Hello? I know you're there."

Not a sound, just squeaking floorboards. "My name is Sierra, and I just want you to know that I am not here to hurt you. None of us want to hurt you or scare you. I'm sorry if we've done that. We are only here to get the truth. We only want to help you."

Like any decent investigator, I waited for a response even though I wasn't really expecting one. These spirits didn't want to talk to me. Not yet. I wanted to give the ghosts a chance to communicate if that's what they wanted, but nobody said a word. I heard nothing but the creaking of the house all around me. Man, this place was noisy. Why was every place I stepped creaking in this house? There were some seriously creaky boards at Brady Hall.

"That mirror crashing to the ground was a good trick. You really got me with that one, but that's not necessary. Are you trying to tell me you want me to have seven years of bad luck? Are you trying to tell me you want me to leave? I can't leave because Bonita is afraid. It would be really great if you would stop scaring her. But you can talk to me if you want. I can help you." Another pause met with silence. "My team is coming in now. Please don't harm them or threaten them. We're only here to help."

As I walked down the stairs, I glanced toward the kitchen just in time to see the skirts of a white dress disappearing around the corner. Naturally, I hurried to see who it was, but there was nothing there. Nothing at all.

I faintly heard the light, pretty laughter of a young girl.

Game on.

I opened the front door and waved the team inside.

Time to get this show on the road.

Chapter Twelve—Sierra

With Helen's new evidence and the fact that I couldn't forget Rose's referral to this part of our investigation as a "stage," we decided to begin night two in the former auditorium or what Bonita called the multipurpose room. It was a large area and had the tendency to produce weird echoes, but it was the perfect location for tonight's focus. The dead that were here—if they were here—Adeo and Elizabeth Monterro, used to perform on the stage nightly for an excited audience. From what we had experienced in the past, actors rarely gave up the spotlight. Not willingly. This tactic worked at the Crescent Theater, and we had good results by pretending to be interested in seeing a play.

Bruce went to the trouble of dressing up in period clothing and even laid out props that were supposedly relevant to another popular play from around the same time. There were no known copies of *Ode to Rebecca*, but we gave it a shot. Surely they would be familiar with *Yellow Bird*, another celebrated stage show from around that time. Bruce cleared his throat nervously as he clutched a few printed pages in his hand. With a flashlight in one hand and the paper in the other, he began his performance. I kept the SLS camera fixed on Bruce as Helen carefully placed her audio recorder on the table near him. She tiptoed back to her chair and offered some applause. Joshua was holding the infrared camera, panning the room slowly.

Here goes nothing. Break a leg, everyone!

As Bruce paused for dramatic flair, Helen clapped again like an enthusiastic fangirl. I played along and cheered as well, but I had to hold the camera steady. I prayed we would attract somebody's attention, but so far we weren't getting any results. Bruce spoke with the bravado of a showman and paced the floor as he did his best to do *Yellow Bird* justice.

It was a good thing Bruce hadn't gone into acting. He wasn't great at it. He paused in weird places, kind of like Shatner, and I glanced around the room thinking he'd spotted something behind me, but there was nothing there. Our Bruce was merely a very bad actor. Helen kept him on track with her occasional excited clapping.

"Bruce! I mean, Mr. Monterro. We need an encore! Encore!" I shouted loudly as I kept the SLS focused on Bruce.

Helen joined me in encouraging him. "Please, Mr. Monterro! We are your biggest fans!"

Within a few seconds of our mentioning the former owner, a figure mapped out on the screen. It shone pink and had long arms and legs. The stick figure wasn't as tall as Bruce, not that he was very tall to begin with, but the being's arms moved erratically. Almost angrily. I got the feeling that somebody did not like us using Mr. Monterro's name.

I didn't have to say a word to Joshua, because he had been peeking over my shoulder when the SLS grabbed the first image. "Keep going, Mr. Monterro. We want that encore!" Joshua encouraged Bruce to continue with applause and a whistle.

"Take this fair maiden, you who stands before this crowd of witnesses. You are no innocent! Listen to me, all! I accuse her of being no genteel flower, no docile turtledove! She is the most wanton of creatures. A trickster with pinkest lips!" Bruce was really getting into his role as an actor, and now there were two figures on the SLS, one on either side of him.

"Look at that!" I whispered like a freight train. "There are two anomalies, Bruce. One to your left and one on the right. Hey, are you okay?" I thought for a second that he'd paused because he'd run out of script, but he looked a little wobbly on his feet. Helen noticed too.

"Bruce?" Helen said with some concern in her voice. I stared at the screen in horror as the two figures appeared to be pummeling Bruce.

"Yikes. I feel a little worse for wear. What's happening? I can feel cold on my right side. Pain too. Like I'm being stabbed. Maybe that's a bit over the top, but that's how I feel."

Helen picked up her audio device and held it close to Bruce.

"I hate to tell you this, but that's exactly what I'm seeing on the SLS. The one on the right appears much more aggressive, and he or she is wailing on you. The shorter figure...oh, it's gone. No, wait. It is back, hovering nearby. Do you need to step away from there? I don't want you to get hurt."

Bruce shook his head defiantly. "I am Mr. Adeo Monterro, and this is my big performance. I need a minute to prepare for my final act!" he declared bravely with a big grin. Now both the figures went crazy and then disappeared.

The four of us immediately clustered together to talk about what just happened. We were getting activity but nothing specific, nothing that proved these figures were relevant to Brady Hall's tragic past or its former occupants. We began exchanging ideas and reviewing evidence, but all that was cut short when an atrocious crashing sound shook the whole building. Immediately we hurried toward the front parlor, but I didn't take off in a full run, not like Joshua and Helen. I'd experienced this phenomenon before. That horrible sound was just like the crashing mirror I heard, but there would be nothing broken. As I brought up the rear of the line that poured into the front room, a blast of wind rushed past me. Only for a brief moment. *Oh, how cold!* So cold that I caught my breath for a few seconds. I remembered to breathe as I panned the camera around, but I caught nothing.

"This is what I heard last night. Sounded just like this huge mirror crashed to the floor, but look—it hasn't moved. It's not even crooked," I commented as the rest of the team attempted to figure out the source of the crash.

"We should check around and make sure everything is intact. Could it have been a window breaking?" Helen suggested as she studied the mirror intently.

"Let's do some EVP work, Helen. Do you have that recorder?"

She shook her white head and snapped her fingers. "Nope. Left it in the other room. I'll go get it." I followed her into the hallway to keep an eye out for her, but my attention was drawn to the stairs. To the top of the stairs, more specifically. A young woman fluttered like an old piece of film, her face as pale as a sheet of paper. Her dark blond hair was piled on top of her head, her mouth set in a stern frown.

Go away!

I didn't hear her words in my ears but in my mind. *Wow, she's powerful*, I thought.

"Why? Why should I go away?"

The woman turned away with a look of disgust—at least her body turned away, but her head did not move with it. She certainly wasn't alive. No living human could twist their neck like that. Maybe only once. I was standing there open-mouthed when Helen joined me.

"Hey, I think there's something on here. The light is flashing. What is it, Sierra?"

"I saw a woman standing there at the top of the stairs. You didn't see anything?"

Helen paused and stared at the now-empty space. "Should we go up there?"

I couldn't believe I was saying this, but I answered her cautiously, "I'm not sure, Helen. I'm really not sure." After a few seconds, I said, "What the heck? There's no time like the present. Hey, Joshua. Bruce. We're going upstairs."

As the men joined us in the hallway, Helen said in an excited tone, "Sierra saw a woman standing there on the landing. We're going up."

"What about the mirror?" Joshua asked as he craned his neck to see what was happening on the second floor.

"That sound is a trick to draw us away from the real action. And here is a question for you: Why are mirrors always such hot items for theaters? Remember at the Crescent? Remember what happened to the Winters lady? I think the entity or entities here could be using the mirrors, traveling through them. We need to see if there are any other mirrors up here."

This was a half-cocked plan, but it was better than no plan. I hoped.

"What do you mean, Sierra? Traveling through the mirrors? What gives you that impression?" Joshua asked as we hustled up the staircase waving our cameras and equipment in all directions. It was pitch black up here.

"I hate to say it—you know I hate to say it—but that's just the feeling I get. I feel like she's using the mirrors to get around."

Helen had broken out the EMF detector and was sweeping it slowly back and forth in the hallway in front of us. There were the occasional blips, but nothing spectacular manifested. Nothing happened on the SLS or the infrared camera, either.

"Are you talking about Elizabeth? You think she's using the mirrors?" Even as Helen asked the question, I felt a sense of wrongness. Like I wasn't getting it quite right.

"I think it would be wrong for us to assume that the apparition seen in the mirror was Elizabeth. There is also a child here and the young woman with the dark circles under her eyes. I don't think Elizabeth was as young as the woman I saw, but who knows? Let's just see if we can make contact and look for any other mirrors. I want to cover every mirror we find except the one downstairs. Maybe we can trap her."

A knocking on the ceiling caught everyone's attention. We tried some EVP work but couldn't get any other knocks or sounds. Bruce agreed with me on the mirror idea. "Obviously, an intelligent spirit doesn't want us to cover the mirrors. This could work. By covering the mirrors, we are limiting her travel. Is that what you mean? Isn't that how it works?"

"Theoretically, yes. We're about to find out."

We ransacked the linen closet in the bathroom and grabbed some sheets to use as mirror covers. We covered the mirror in the bathroom, the mirror in the downstairs bathroom and two mirrors upstairs in the bedrooms. After our work, we descended into the front parlor and waited. I gave Helen the SLS and took the digital recorder. Everyone backed away as I stood in front of the mirror alone. We lit a candle as a kind of trigger object, and I set it on the table behind me. It cast strange shadows on the walls around me.

I did not pause to wonder why this felt like such a personal attack. I didn't question it. It happened occasionally. No, this woman didn't want me at Brady Hall, and she had cleverly hidden from everyone else. But we'd seen her a few times. She had been one of the figures on the screen and one of the momentary blips on the infrared footage we'd captured in the upstairs hallway; we were all so frustrated by her elusiveness. I wasn't willing to give up yet, though.

This was my Hail Mary pass. This was all I had to give.

I clicked the ON button on the audio recorder and placed it on the table beneath the mirror. "This is Sierra in front of the mirror in the parlor. The second night of the investigation." Glancing at my watch, I added, "It is 11:45 p.m." As I waited for the team to get settled in their spots, I stared into the blackness of the mirror. I focused all my attention on the emptiness. I was going to make contact, there was no question of that, but with what? I was not yet sure. An angry ghost? A darker entity masquerading as a young woman? The possibilities were endless.

"I know you are here. I can feel you. There's no sense in hiding from me because there's nowhere to go. I've covered all the mirrors. You can't go anywhere. You can't leave and hide. We have to talk."

I heard Joshua catch his breath right before I saw her. I hadn't realized that I'd closed my eyes for a second. The mirror was reflecting my face and the faces of my team members, but there was also another face cast in black and white and mostly in shadow, like a living, breathing photograph. No, not living. Not breathing. The woman in the mirror stood off to the side, her face turned away from me slightly.

"Look at me. I can see you. I know you're there." But she did not move, nor did she acknowledge my presence. She was still, like a mannequin, as I took in the details of her profile.

No, this was not Elizabeth.

This woman resembled the first sketch that Cassidy sent me yesterday. The Gibson Girl woman. The one she called a murderess. "Tell me your name. Tell me your name so I can help you." The only response to my request was a low and rumbly whisper before she backed away. I reached for the audio recorder and played back the sound.

Adeo...

She vanished right before my eyes, but I still felt her very near. Yes, she was in the mirror, but I could not force her to step out or talk to me. She was stubborn, this one.

We tried for hours, but no other activity occurred at Brady Hall. The team appeared defeated, but I reminded them again that most investigations were built on the things we didn't know we captured until the review.

"Let's wrap it, guys. I think this is it for the night. We've got a busy day ahead of us with lots of evidence to review. I'm going to need all hands on deck tomorrow. Anyone who's free, please give a girl a hand. Let's take a look at the camera footage first. We need to get answers for Bonita, and quickly."

I left the house exhausted, but I would never forget the woman's face. And I finally knew her name. She gave me that much, at least, but that was all. And she was still looking for Adeo. I wondered who she had been to him. What had been her role in all that happened here?

Goodbye, Lynette.

You haven't seen the last of me, though. I'll be back with a friend.

I locked the door and left Brady Hall.

Chapter Thirteen—Lynette

It was standing room only at Broussards. I recognized many of the faces, many of our regular patrons, but this wasn't necessarily unusual. The theater folk did love their plays and performances. But who had ever heard of a sold-out Thursday show? Apparently, people loved this particular play because dozens of souls packed into the tiny space to see it. Yes, people were often fascinated with shiny new things.

I was not familiar with the playwright, or even many of the actors, but I had every intention of getting a peek at the actress listed on the playbill. The one who'd apparently stolen Adeo's heart.

Her name was Ruby Alexandria. Obviously, this was a stage name, but it wasn't strange to take such a flamboyant moniker. People liked to hide their boring upbringings behind clever names, didn't they? Perhaps that was my problem. I hadn't figured out a suitable stage name. Nobody was going to be impressed by the name Lynette Farris. That was not the name of a notable actress.

Before I met Adeo, I never imagined that I could be anything other than a seamstress, but he had seen something in me. A glimmer of brilliance, he called it. In the beginning, I read for him, filling in the gaps when Elizabeth was unwell or otherwise unavailable to run lines. Actual stage performances were rare for me, but I had a few opportunities to wear the yellow dress and sing the trills as Lucrezia. The newspapers declared me to be "an exciting new find." I expected to have more time on stage after that glowing review, but to my disappointment, quite the opposite happened. I assumed Elizabeth considered me to be too much of a threat to her own role. Yes, she was the playwright. *Ode to Rebecca* had been her brainchild, but I had made it come alive! Adeo wholeheartedly agreed with me, but he never promised to do anything about it. His advice to me had been to be patient and wait for my big break.

I had no patience, and I could see no break coming. Not for Lynette Farris.

Not unless I made it happen!

Ronald adored me, but we were not the same caliber person. Ronald wanted to find a wife and settle down on a farm. None of his domestic vision appealed to me. The only person I ever wanted to belong to was Adeo, and he routinely crushed my dreams beneath his elegant black bootheels.

But it couldn't be him! It couldn't be my lover. It must be Elizabeth who demanded such a thing! Adeo loved me. He loved me well enough for all these months. He loved me when I was sick and even brought me soup and some medicines. Even the rest of the crew knew of our affections for one another.

Until recently, he had been kind and considerate, but all that had changed; how quickly he changed! No! It must be Elizabeth! Adeo had no choice in the matter, which seemed strange to me because Adeo was such a strong man with a strong will and spirit. That was one of the things I loved most about him.

Oh, yes. I loved him. With all my heart and as well as I could.

But here I was at Broussards lining up against the wall with the other peons because it was standing room only tonight. On a Thursday! Like all these others, I hoped to watch the performance of the celebrated Miss Ruby Alexandria.

As soon as she stepped out onto the stage, my heart sank. Ruby was tall and shapely like a Greek statue in a fitted costume. Her hair was light brown, the kind of brown that was genuinely beautiful. It shimmered in the stage light. She wore no feathers in her hair because she didn't need them. My heart ached at her loveliness.

It can't be true. It can't be true that Adeo loves this woman.

I wanted to throw up. I even put my hand to my mouth.

What about me? Why was he so eager to leave me behind? I had been enough for him before.

The play began, and at first, I was unimpressed. Clearly, the woman had a voice that was too high; the orchestra was out of tune and the piece nothing but silliness. She began some monologue about peacocks and golden birds. What tripe! No, I must have this all wrong. It couldn't be true. Ronald was having me on. I clutched my bonnet and decided I would leave and return to Brady Hall. I didn't belong here. I had so much work to do, and this was a waste of my time. Later tonight, I would go in search of Adeo, and we would talk of our future. I would find him and tell him the truth about my feelings.

I would not allow him to say goodbye to me. He could never let me go. I would not allow such a thing.

But then the world stopped. I saw nothing but the man in front of me. I heard nothing, for my eyes were locked on my own love, who was sitting in the audience. His sleek black hair was carefully combed, his mustache beautifully oiled. I could only see him from the side, but there was no mistaking him.

"Adeo," I whispered to myself. I should run to him, shake him and demand that he leave with me now, but it would do me no good. My eyes were now focused on the beautiful Ruby Alexandria, whose voice suddenly became the sweetest sound I had ever heard. As she lifted her voice higher and then lower, she sang every note perfectly and climbed the trills perfectly. From high to low and back again, from one note to another, she captivated her audience like a brilliant sorceress. Adeo and the rest of the audience were on their feet clapping; their faces swept up in the rapture as the first act came to an end. How long had I been watching him?

Time had sped by as my heart broke into a thousand pieces. As the curtain fell and the thunderous applause continued, I experienced earth-shattering defeat. Yes, for the first time, I knew I had been defeated.

Adeo would never be mine, and he would never be Elizabeth's. Adeo was a man with love enough only for himself.

I pushed out of the small auditorium and stumbled onto the street. I clutched a wooden post as I tried to catch my breath. Ronald had been right all along. Adeo never intended to marry me or to treat me right. I was nothing to him. Nothing at all. He'd told me as much, but I hadn't believed him. He'd made it clear, but I had been so blind.

As I stood there listening to the music tinkling out of Broussards, I gritted my teeth.

Fine. If he's not going to be with me, he won't be with anyone. He would never be unfaithful ever again. I would see to that. I knew just what to do.

By the time I made it back to Brady Hall, I had the plan perfected in my mind. There would be no chance that I would fail this time. No chance that I would stumble. As I opened the door, I came face to face with myself in the grand, gold-framed mirror.

I wept as I took in my own haggard appearance. It was quiet in the parlor. There was no one here but me. All the players and production folks had taken the night off to do whatever it was that happy people did. Elizabeth would be upstairs scribbling and crying over her latest creation, but other than her, I was alone at Brady Hall. Even Mortie, the cook, had taken a day off.

Always alone. Alone again.

Adeo, why? I cried as my hand rested on the mirror. My face was pressed against the coolness of the glass, as if I could embrace myself, to give myself some solace.

Then it happened. I hadn't expected it. I couldn't have guessed it. But it happened.

A small, rather pale hand reached out of the mirror and held mine. It was cold, colder than the icehouse. I did not pull away. I did not flinch as the hand clutched mine. This was what I wanted. I did everything Mortie suggested to catch the spirit who fluttered about in the glass. Although Mortie did not approve, she happily took my money in exchange for her information.

The little girl spoke to me, to my mind. She knew what I wanted to do. She knew it all. And she promised to help me. She would be mine, and I would be hers.

Finally, I knew I was not alone. I would never be alone again.

And neither would Rebecca.

Chapter Fourteen—Cassidy

"Look, Emily. Mommy is a popular girl this week. First Aunt Helen and now Aunt Cassidy stopped by for a visit, all in a space of two days." Sierra opened the door with a defeated smile and gave me a hug. Her eyes were sporting circles that were even darker than usual. Emily cried on her hip, and every fantasy I may have had about motherhood disappeared like shadows on a cloudy day.

Nope, I'm not ready for that. Not one bit.

"Hey, Sierra. Hey, Emily. Is this a bad time?"

She carefully avoided my question and waved me inside. "When did you get into town? Is this about Midas? Come in, please, but be warned—it's Crazy Town Central at my house."

"I bet it is with a baby and two dogs to manage."

"And Joshua," she added. "I swear my husband is a big ol' man-child. Can't find a hamper to save his life. Can't make a sandwich for himself. I blame myself...and Mrs. McBride for babying him so much. Big Brother not with you?"

I smiled at her and tried not to take that personally. I didn't begrudge them their friendship. That wouldn't be right. "Not this time, but he sends his love. He's going to call you later or maybe come by. He went by to see Papa Angelos. He's had a tough go of it lately with his health. We thought about staying another day in Gulf Shores, but he was concerned about his grandfather. He's pressuring me to set a date for the wedding.

He's worried that Papa won't be...well enough to attend. But guess what?"

"Don't make me guess," she replied as she put the baby in her walker. Emily just kind of sat there, her chubby legs dangling down. She stared at me and then her mother. At least she'd stopped crying. I sat on the floor beside Emily and began putting toys on her walker tray. That perked her up.

"I sold all of my paintings! Can you believe that? And they asked me to come back next year. I loved every minute of it, Sierra. I wasn't sure I would, but I did."

She hugged me and rubbed the top of my head with her hand. Like I was another one of her kids. "That is the best news! You and Midas are getting along, and everything really is kosher?" Sierra asked as she collapsed on the couch beside me. Sherman walked in and rubbed his cold nose against me.

"Yep. We're great. Hey, Sherm. Have you been a good boy?" The white-haired dog wagged his tail and showed his pink tongue as if to convince me that indeed he had been a good boy. Naturally, I thought of Jocelyn whenever I hung out with him. She'd be happy to see him looking so healthy and content.

"Don't believe that. You see that Bozo isn't coming anywhere near me. In the past two days, these two miscreants have destroyed my beanbag chair and all my throw pillows. I don't know what has gotten into them lately. They act like heathens, and then Emily's been cranky every day this week. God, I wish her teeth would come in already. Sorry. I just kind of piled it on, didn't I?"

I put the keys back on Emily's walker tray. Apparently, throwing them down for me to pick up was some kind of cool baby game. "How is the investigation going, if you don't mind me asking? Did you find out anything about the women in the sketches?" I ditched my book bag on the floor beside me but kept an eye on Sherman. I didn't need him tearing my worn bag to pieces. He moseyed away now that he'd been outed for his bad behavior. Such a funny dog. A dog with an old soul.

"It has really been a strange one. Usually, I am much more intuitive, but connecting with these entities has been a challenge. I feel kind of discombobulated. It's just weird." We sat in silence and watched Emily play. It felt peaceful here, despite the chaos that accompanied playful dogs and an occasionally crying baby.

Eventually, Sierra began sharing what she'd experienced, and I listened intently as she revealed what she'd discovered from the team's investigation of Brady Hall. I was amazed at the parallels between this theater and the one on Dauphin Street.

"The mirror is significant here as well. I'll have to do some more research about this phenomenon because it's clear that mirrors are more powerful than we suspected. Or at least I suspected," I added thoughtfully.

Sierra tugged at her messy ponytail. "From everything we've gathered, Adeo Monterro, the victim, was not a particularly scrupulous guy when it came to the ladies. He had his hands on every woman who walked past him. And like many such men, once he made his conquest, he was ready to move on. From what I can gather, Elizabeth, his wife, had secrets too, but I don't believe she killed her husband."

A hollow place began to form in my stomach. When was the last time I'd eaten? I'd been skipping meals too regularly lately. I didn't have the stomach to eat much of anything.

Except for avocados. I couldn't get enough of them. Once Midas turned me onto avocado toast, I was in love.

"That would go along with what I've been drawing as well. I think that Brady Hall has been an unhappy place exposed to serious emotional turmoil for a long time. I think the most likely scenario is that the client triggered the activity when she got there and started moving things around; with all that unwanted activity, the house, meaning the spirits in the house, sprang back to life for lack of a better phrase. It's almost as if she has drawn them back there."

Sierra bit her bottom lip and rubbed Sherman's head. He'd placed his fuzzy face in her lap while Bozo growled disapprovingly from the doorway.

"I think that's probably true. Bonita is under a lot of stress to sell that building, And from the little bit of information I have about her personal life—I don't guess she would mind me repeating this—she survived a messy divorce. She didn't say this, but I hear from my mother-in-law that the Realtor market is tougher than I imagined. Pretty cutthroat, actually. But I haven't told you the best part. Or perhaps the worst part. This happened to the team and me last night at the very end before everything went quiet."

Sierra relayed to me the results of her interaction with the spirit in the mirror. She floored me with her description of those events. I couldn't wait any longer to show her my work.

"You're just going to die when you see this, Sierra. This was my sketch from last night. It's a girl, stronger than the grown women who haunt the place. And the sad thing is, she is not quite human anymore." I couldn't pull out the sketchpad quickly enough. I immediately began flipping to last night's feverish sketch.

Sierra didn't say anything at first as she held the sketch in both hands. She studied it in silence. It was an odd drawing, but the images were powerful. The woman hugging the glass, the spirit reaching out.

"I think I understand what this means," I began cautiously. "This mirror is being used as a portal for the spirits at Brady Hall. During Lynette's time, a dead child reached out to her when she was at her most vulnerable, and somehow she made a strong connection with that spirit. It was so strong that the thing influenced this woman to do murder."

"You're calling her a thing. She's a dead girl. How can she be a thing?" Sierra asked without hiding her disgust for that choice of words.

Wow, my friend was really stressed out.

I picked up Emily's keys again and then accepted my drawing back from Sierra.

"She *was* a girl, but now she is not. She orchestrated the murder. She did that. She will do it again if she can—if she's allowed to. That's what I mean when I say she is a thing. She's not a child. Not anymore. All she can think of is revenge, Sierra."

Sierra rubbed her eyes and tugged at her ponytail again. "This is much worse than I thought. I've been reviewing footage this morning, and there's nothing to see. Not an EVP, not an image, not much of anything. A few blips. I saw a shadow person and a brief reflection in the mirror, but there's nothing to show the client. Most everything I've seen has been a personal experience, not evidence. What do we tell Bonita?"

I tapped my fingers on my book bag as I thought about it for a minute. I already knew the answer to this question, but I wanted Sierra to come to it on her own. She needed to understand it because this was about her. The spirits had targeted her, one in particular. It had a thing about mommies. It wanted revenge. Sierra was a mommy.

"How did you feel when you were at Brady Hall?" I smiled at her to reassure her that I wasn't criticizing her.

"What do you mean?"

"It's not a trick question. How did you feel when you were in the house? Emotionally. Tell me what you were feeling, first thoughts."

She covered herself with her Alabama throw blanket. "I felt targeted, personally targeted. I felt like whoever was there didn't want me around, and they knew I was coming. And then Rose told me that the spirits there were mistaken about my intentions. I kind of brushed it off after that."

"Did she? What else did she say?" I'd never met Rose, but according to Midas, she was an interesting person with a mysterious past.

"We had an interesting conversation, for sure. Rose said I needed to talk to the spirits and let them know that I wasn't coming to harm them, that I only wanted to talk. I did that, though I don't know how much good it did. I feel terrible that there's a little girl trapped there. This just makes me sick."

"Sierra Kay McBride, listen to me. The little girl is not a little girl anymore. You have to get that through your head. Please. You'll only beat yourself up. She died over a hundred and fifty years ago. What is left of her, whatever fragments remain behind, want nothing from us except revenge."

"Revenge for what?" Sierra asked as my skin crackled with electricity.

"You don't get it yet? You must really be tired, Sierra. I'm sorry. Her mother was Elizabeth. This girl is Rebecca. She is what it's all about. This is the crime that Elizabeth was trying to hide from everyone. But Rebecca wouldn't let it go. And she wanted revenge so much; she wanted it so much that she became evil. I know that doesn't fit with our thinking about children, but it is the truth and we have to banish her. She'll never punish enough mommies. She doesn't understand that her mother is gone now."

"So, nobody's innocent here? There are no good guys, just bad guys. Nobody we can help? That's it, isn't it? They're all dead bad guys."

I held her hands, as I understood how tired and burdened she was. "Sometimes paranormal investigation isn't black and white; isn't that what you told me? I know you want it to be, especially in this case, but it's just not. We have to help them move on, all of them. Innocent or not."

"She didn't deserve what happened to her. Her own mother?" Sierra swallowed back tears as she glanced at Emily, who was blowing spit bubbles and playing with her plastic toy keys.

"And nobody deserves to be lost for eternity either. We can help Rebecca by sending her on her way, whether she wants to go or not. She can't stay, Sierra. You know that. We don't have to do it today, but we need to do it soon."

"Today. It should be today. Will you help me go through the evidence? I need to change Emily and feed her and..."

I hugged her, and she collapsed on my shoulder. Sierra rarely cried. I took it as proof that our friendship had reached such a mature place that she trusted me enough to show her emotions.

"I'll order us some lunch and run through the evidence. I'll be right here. And when you're ready, whether it's an hour from now or ten hours from now, we'll go. Together. Okay?"

"Thanks, Cassidy. I'll be glad for the help." She reached for a tissue from the box beside her and dabbed her tears away.

"You're not Super Woman, Sierra. No matter what you tell yourself. You need other people. Just like I do." She wrinkled her nose at that idea and frowned at me before flashing her knowing smile. "Okay, you don't need them much, but you do need them. And don't thank me yet. I think we've still got a battle on our hands."

"What's that smell? Oh...ooh, Emily." She scooped up Emily to change her stinky diaper. "At least I won't have to fight that battle by myself. Hey, how do you feel about diaper changing?"

"Uh..." I smiled sheepishly. "Ambivalent? Uninterested?"

"Good call," she said with a laugh as she carried her smelly child to her bedroom.

I flipped open my laptop and logged onto the Gulf Coast Paranormal server. We kind of knew how this was going to go, but it wouldn't be right to skip over the evidence. Midas taught us to always review everything. Always. And that's exactly what I planned to do.

Time to get this party started.

Chapter Fifteen—Elizabeth

Just minutes before I was to take my place on the stage, I realized I could not breathe. Clearly, Lynette had cinched my gown too tightly. The fabric felt stiff and unyielding. I should have never agreed to this new demand of Adeo's, to make her my personal wardrobe mistress. She served as my understudy already; surely this additional role would be of no interest to her. But she came to my dressing room like an obedient cow. Just as I was an obedient cow.

Obedient to whatever commands Adeo gave me.

At least she knew where she stood now. He had broken it off with her, just as I begged him to do. Oh dear, this would never do. Was it too late to change back into my blue gown? What would Adeo say if I strolled out onto the stage wearing my dress from the previous act?

But I asked her to give me more room about the chest and waist. I would fire her for this! I did not care one whit about the repercussions. This kind of thing could not be ignored. This was a very demanding role, particularly this new, final scene, but evidently, the young woman was determined to destroy me.

The dress had been much more comfortable at my last fitting. I was not growing fatter, as Lynette hinted at numerous times. My gowns were shrinking, thanks to the homewrecking trollop, Lynette Farris. Was my husband's rejected lover deliberately trying to sabotage me? Yes. Everyone was against me. I heard the whispers. I knew what they said about Adeo. He had another lover, but what cared I? He'd had a hundred before Lynette. Maybe I would take a lover, too.

Someone whispered behind me, and I waved the sound away as if it were a mosquito buzzing in my ear. Even my own husband was against me. I had always known Adeo was a weak man, but I thought surely he would change. That my beloved plays would impress him. *Oh, how he used to love my mind.*

He would never change, though—he made that clear as he revealed the truth. He knew my horrible secret. He knew about Rebecca and Benjamin and all the ones who came before. Adeo knew and had always known, but he did not know everything. No, he did not know everything.

I bit my knuckle to remind myself to abide in this moment. Just this one.

But his words I could never forget. Not in a million years. When Adeo whispered my secrets, when he said them aloud, my heart experienced such pain, as if he had reached into my chest and pulled the beating thing out. I had been hiding for weeks, but now I had to perform this new scene. The very role that I had begged for, pleaded for, the very one that I had been singularly obsessed with.

Adding this scene had cost me everything. But I had to go on. I had to make this one further sacrifice.

What am I thinking? Why am I here? I could easily leave Adeo, leave it all behind, but what would that garner me? No. *Ode to Rebecca* was all I had left. I would do the scene if it was the last scene I did.

A tap on my shoulder from a bored-looking stagehand reminded me that this was my cue. Immediately, my cold hand reached into my gown's pocket and grasped the cold metal. I palmed the knife as we practiced and raised my free hand to roaring applause as I began my dialogue. This was a confrontational scene, one that required an immense amount of emotion.

Before I stepped onto the stage, I was not absolutely sure I would be able to pull the dialogue or song off. I doubted that I could make this play come alive, but now there was no Elizabeth.

Only Lucrezia.

And Rebecca.

Rebecca?

I didn't move, and the words were caught in my throat. Ignoring Adeo's handsome face, I stared past my husband. Rebecca! Yes, I would know my own daughter! Her hair was so short, but I remembered that I cut it before she died; the lice had been so bad. She kept bringing lice home, so I cut it...I cut it all off. She had cried over her hair. As I looked at her now, her hair was short and plastered to her head because she was wet from head to toe. Her nightgown was also drenched through as if she had just been pulled out of the pond.

Just as she had been that day. Oh, my own heart!

All the world grew silent. "Rebecca? Is that you?" I whispered to the luminous child that flickered and vanished from my view. Only her soft, sweet voice remained.

You'll die too, Mother. You'll die too.

The scene had grown black and as silent as the grave until Adeo's face breached my view. His painted eyes and lips were bright, clownish. He was saying my name, repeating my name. Not Elizabeth but Lucrezia. I looked out at the audience. Oh dear, I had missed my cue, but Adeo was coming back around. He was improvising to provide me time to get back into the heat of the moment.

I could not let him down. Could I?

I had no other thought. I had no thought other than to stab him. Just as I was expected to do. That was what came next, wasn't it? It was for the play, at least. Not because anger overwhelmed me. Not because the animal inside me took over and wanted to choke whatever living thing stood before me. Not because of that.

There were more lines, but I forgot them. The only thing I knew was that I had the knife in my hand. With a savage scream, I plunged the thing into his chest not once or twice but many times. To my surprise, the blade did not click back as it was supposed to. Instead, it slid through Adeo's bone and flesh; it felt as if I had pierced a watermelon. A warm, bloody watermelon. I screamed as the blood surged from his body like a furious fountain.

What is happening?
What have I done?
This isn't right.

This wasn't right at all. The knife slipped from my hand and fell to the wooden stage floor with a clatter. Sticky, warm blood covered my palm and my fingers as it crept down my arm in long rivulets.

What have I done? Confused by all of the activity, I slowly rose to my feet, but Adeo did not rise with me. The thunderous roar of the crowd surprised me as onlookers stood to their feet and clapped furiously. I waited and waited, but the applause continued and Adeo did not move.

Soon a few stagehands came to his aid, and I watched absently as the audience went quiet. At least I could breathe now. I could breathe. I could hear the creaking of corsets and the nervous tapping of shoes and all the whispers.

Oh no! They figured it out. They figured out the trick. They saw the truth. They knew everything. They knew it all. Everyone knew!

I thought I would cry or beg for mercy, but I did not. I laughed instead. I laughed like a madwoman, long and loud. I can't say why I laughed, but I tucked my right foot behind my left and elegantly lifted the hem of my skirts. *Oh dear. That blood will ruin this gown.* But the bloodstains didn't shock me, for I felt nothing. Only laughter and ruin.

Such a strange combination.

And then her eyes met mine. Not Rebecca's but Lynette's. Her eyes sparkled like those of a deer that had been transfixed by the light. I had seen that happen before when we lived on the farm. Rebecca and Benjamin and me. We had all been together.

Lynette's eyes sparkled just like that sweet-faced doe. Oh, but I had not taken her by surprise. There was no shock on her face at all. Nothing but pure satisfaction.

As the theater turned to chaos, I laughed even harder as I witnessed my husband's mistress fleeing Brady Hall. Oh, she'd been a clever girl. She had been far cleverer than me, but I had this moment. I had this moment in the spotlight.

And that's all I had left.

Lynette had murdered my soul.

Chapter Sixteen—Sierra

"Bonita says the activity in the house has really kicked up. I'm glad we're going back. I hope we can help her. I'd hate to think we made the situation worse," I confessed as we pulled into the empty parking space.

"What's happening?" Cassidy asked as she unhooked her seat belt. "What kind of activity?"

I put my keys in my purse. "Footprints. Watery footprints all over the house. It's so bad that she called in a plumber to check it out, but there's no source. She says it looks just like somebody stepped out of the shower and took a walk through the house. It really scared her. No one is living in the house, so no one is using the shower, and there's no swimming pool."

Cassidy shook her head in disbelief. "Wow. I guess you're right; it is a good thing we're here. The good news is I don't think Elizabeth wants to be here. Lynette is the wild card, though. I'm not sure if they are even aware of each other at this point."

"Yeah, they are, and I think the hate between Elizabeth and Lynette continues. Do you really think Rebecca is...something else? God, I don't want to believe that. I know it can happen, souls can fracture, can become all sorts of things, but I don't know. The fact that it is a child, a little girl...."

"I don't know how to explain it all. Maybe I am wrong, Sierra. You are better at sorting this kind of stuff out. I could be completely wrong, but I don't think there's anything left of Rebecca. At this point, she's just a shadow. That little girl is gone. It's just a bit of her that's left, but that bit is strong and so angry."

My heart broke to hear her words, and I was quietly determined to help this child. Murdered and abandoned. Left fractured and lashing out. All words that should not be used to describe a child. It was disgusting.

Bonita quickly left after letting us in. I wasn't sure if she was coming back anytime soon, but I had a feeling this was going to take a little while. Helping Elizabeth would be easy—Cassidy was right about that. Lynette would be a little tougher, but I was pretty sure that if Adeo was around, he wouldn't put up much of a fight. There was no evidence to support the idea that he was still here, but the child was another story.

Rebecca deserved to have her story told, but if it was as Cassidy said, Rebecca didn't understand she was dead. If she didn't know that what she was doing was wrong, then it might be a struggle.

Neither one of us spoke much as we walked inside the house. We stood before the mirror and stared at our reflections. Why was I so anxious? Cassidy shivered beside me and briefly squeezed my hand. Her skin was icy cold.

"It's not just me? Thank goodness. Spirits definitely use this mirror. They come in and out of this thing. It's like a full-blown portal, but no one is in there right now."

I closed my eyes and focused on "feeling" the presence of Others. *Nothing down here, nothing outside. Ah, that's where they are hiding.* "They're all in the attic. Only there's not much of an attic up there, so I don't know how we will navigate that.

They're hiding from us, and we need to confront them. All of them."

Her eyes watched me in the mirror. "We best go up and get started, then," Cassidy said dryly. I noticed she hadn't carried her book bag or any of her investigative tools with her. No need for that. We knew there were ghosts here; what we didn't know was how to help them. Hopefully, we would find a way.

"Let's do it." We left the front parlor, traveled up the stairs to the attic and somehow managed to pull the ladder down. The ceilings were rather high, but Cassidy had strong arms and hoisted me up high enough to reach the pull-down chain. The ladder came down easily, but even as it slid down I could hear a shuffling noise, a kind of weird sort of footsteps.

Nope. That wasn't quite right either. I wasn't sure what to call the sound. Not footsteps, more like the crinkling of fabric.

Like you'd hear in the theater when there was a show about to happen. It was a necessary part of the production to take the dresses out and allow them to breathe, to clean and fluff the material. Yes, that's the sound I was hearing, the rubbing of fabric. But there was simply nothing up here. If there had been a wardrobe storage area up here before, it was certainly not here now.

The two of us sat on the first beam inside the attic. We set up no equipment, no laser grids or REM-pods. We had no audio recorders. We were going on intuition and our senses. We were two mediums, after all. If we couldn't hear the dead at this point, something was wrong with us.

Cassidy nodded at me, and I took a deep breath, remembering to remain calm. "My name is Sierra, and this is my friend Cassidy. Cassidy has been drawing your pictures.

You've been telling her your stories. All of you have been telling your stories to us both. Please, please listen to us. We're here to help you. We don't want to hurt you or harm you in any kind of way. We're only here to bring you peace."

Cassidy agreed with me. "She's telling the truth. We just want to help. Elizabeth? Can you hear me? We know what happened to you. We know what happened to Adeo. We know you didn't mean to kill him, and we believe that you loved him. I don't know about everything else, and I don't have to know, but I do know you cannot stay here any longer. I'm sorry that you are hurt, but this place is for the living. This is not your place. This place belongs to living people now, and you are making them afraid. It is time to leave."

In my mind, I heard her answer Cassidy's command. It was a weak voice that I could barely discern.

This is my place. My place. All of this is mine. She can't have him.

I touched Cassidy's hand to let her know I needed to speak. "Elizabeth, listen to me. Adeo isn't here anymore; he's gone...he's gone through the door. He went to the light—he's not here. By refusing to leave, all you are doing is preventing yourself from going to see him. I know you want to go. I know you want to see Adeo and Rebecca, so I want you to try really hard. I want you to focus on your love for Adeo. Nothing else. Not your guilt, not your regret. Just Adeo. He's waiting for you, Elizabeth."

"Oh, crap. There's Lynette," Cassidy said as she pointed at a shadow that appeared along the far wall. "Hurry up, Sierra."

I whined at the sight. "Elizabeth, now is the time. She can't stop you from seeing Adeo. She can't stop you from going to him. I want you to look for the door; it's about to open. Just look for it."

The sounds of the woman's soft crying didn't melt my heart. This woman, Elizabeth Monterro, had murdered her daughter. She killed her in cold blood. Rebecca deserved her revenge, however that played out.

Cassidy must have sensed my hesitation. She cleared her throat and picked up the dialogue. "Elizabeth, I can promise you that this is not a trick. We want you to be free. We need you to leave this place. I know you love your daughter. I know you loved her. Now prove that love—this is your one chance to prove that you did care about Rebecca."

I heard the ghost of Elizabeth Monterro make a sort of whiny sound, which I interpreted hopefully, like she was considering our offer.

Tears filled my eyes. I had to do this for Rebecca. I had to do this for Bonita. I knew how stressful motherhood could be, but that was no excuse for what happened to Rebecca. Yes, it needed to end. The cycle had to be broken. Right here, right now.

"Please, please, Elizabeth. It isn't right for you to be here, to be tormented like this. You may have done a lot of things in your life, things you would like to keep hidden, but nobody deserves to be kept away from their loved ones forever. Go to the light. I'm opening the door for you." And as I said it, I saw the door opening. "See the door? It's full of light and love. Please, Elizabeth. Step toward it. You see it, don't you? Yes, you do. I see it too." Tears streamed down my face. "It's warm and white, and it envelops you. It's a safe place." Suddenly Cassidy was clutching my hand, tears running down her cheeks. These kinds of transitions were always emotional. And it wasn't lost on me how precious these moments were. How very precious indeed.

And then she was gone. I knew Elizabeth had made her choice. She had slipped through to the other side. And without hesitation, we focused on the next spirit.

This one wasn't going to go without a fight. So be it.

Chapter Seventeen—Sierra

Cassidy touched my hand to let me know that she had this one. I was glad about that because I was exhausted. I hadn't realized until the other night how exhausted I truly was; how very empty. I was looking forward to going to Gulf Shores and reminded myself to thank Cassidy and Midas again for that surprise trip to the beach. The beach always refreshed me.

I wished I could be there right now.

Instead, I was here in this hot attic with this evil, dead girl. But she was still a little girl. I wasn't ready to give up on her. I had to stay focused. I had to stay present in this moment. I visualized a protective blue light around Cassidy. Yeah, I could at least do this much. I let it get cold and then warm, cold and then warm, like it was pulsating.

Wow. That grabbed the dead woman's attention.

Lynette revealed herself, and it was an ugly manifestation of the woman she'd been. She stepped out of a shadowy corner, and her Gibson Girl bun was the only thing I recognized. Her face was a skeletal representation, presumably of herself.

A flood of information came my way, and I began sharing it. This was the only way we could strip her power away and see the truth of who she had been.

"Cassidy, she didn't die here. She's back here because she likes seeing what she's done. She likes thinking that she won. She believes that she is the one responsible for Elizabeth's downfall. She was her mortal enemy—those are her words, not mine. She wants to know why we're here."

"Lynette, you should have known you would not get away with this. It's time to come clean," Cassidy added. "This is Bonita's place now, and she wants you to leave Brady Hall." Cassidy tilted her head and stared in the direction of the creepy corner. I knew she couldn't see Lynette, not with her eyes, but she could feel her. And the feeling of her was dark and ominous and oppressive. But she was still human.

"She captured the little girl. Oh, God!" I began to cry. "She's bragging about it. She did it! Lynette captured Rebecca's spirit. We thought it was the other way around, but actually, she knew about the child and captured her. She used her up, and what's left is this evil thing. Oh my God!" It felt like a kick in the gut. "She's been using her all these years. Lynette has used this child up—she's the one! She took all of her humanity. She's taken all of her and used it against her mother. Oh God!" I couldn't help but weep. Cassidy put her hand on my shoulder.

"Lynette, you don't have any right to be here. Elizabeth is gone. You may have contributed to her death, but you have no power over her now. None at all! She is free, and you're stuck here. You're stuck here, and Adeo has gone on without you."

And then with my ears, I could hear her screaming at us, "I want Adeo!"

Cassidy kept going. "You blew it. You had your chance, but you messed it up. You've lost him forever. He's not here, and he won't come back, not for anyone. He's at peace. He's where he should be, and now you need to go." She didn't promise her anything. Cassidy didn't ascribe her to heaven or hell; that wasn't in our authority. We couldn't open any door for her either. Cassidy didn't promise her that her loved ones would meet her. She simply wasn't giving her a choice.

"You have to go, Lynette. You get out of this house and let Rebecca go. You do not have any rights to her at all. You never did!"

She growled at us and kicked up a low cloud of sawdust. I couldn't see her with my eyes now, but I knew she was creeping closer, and I was concerned about being perched precariously on a ladder. She could easily at any moment just shove us off. She hated all women! Yes, all women, and we were no exception. Didn't we understand that? Didn't we understand that she hated us?

Adeo...bring me Adeo, she warned us again, and then the attic went silent. A sound at the bottom of the stairs caught my attention. How did she circle back around? I didn't see her go past me.

It wasn't like we could trap a ghost in the attic, but normally I sensed their movement, especially once they manifested.

"Hurry and get down," I warned Cassidy. But it wasn't Lynette that I saw. I saw the dingy edge of a child's nightgown and her feet as she glided past the ladder. Who could that be except Rebecca?

Cassidy was the first to climb down. And I was right behind her.

"It's her. It's the child. Lynette doesn't want to let her go. What do you feel, Cassidy? What do you see?"

"Nothing, but my feelings are everywhere. I feel desperation. And fear. Deep and abiding fear."

Standing still, I heard a familiar sound, one I'd grown accustomed to hearing at Brady Hall. The sound of a mirror crashing. The large mirror in the parlor. I hurried to go see it, but there was nothing to see. The mirror was in its place; it was hanging perfectly evenly on the wall, and there were no reflections except our own. We looked terrified and a bit worse for wear.

I heard the child's voice in my ear. I knew exactly what she was saying. What she'd been saying all this time. She'd been telling us how to set her free, and oh, she wanted to leave so desperately. She didn't want to be a creature. No!

Break the mirror!

"What is it?" Cassidy asked me. "What is she saying? I heard a voice, but I can't make it out. It's Rebecca, isn't it? I've got goose pimples on top of my goose pimples. I know something is going on. What is it, Sierra?"

Unblinking, I answered her, "She says we have to break the mirror." It did me no good to whisper, for as soon as I got the words out of my mouth, there was a scream erupting from the staircase accompanied by the heaviest footsteps I'd ever heard in my life. It sounded like an army was stomping down the steps in unison, and each of them took the same step. Oh man, the house was shaking. My heart was about to beat out of my chest, and I knew who was coming for me.

For us!

Lynette was coming.

She was coming to collect the child. She didn't want to let her go.

"You can't have her!" Cassidy shouted. "She's not your daughter! She belongs to her mother. She belongs to

Elizabeth!" Okay, so that probably was not the best thing to say, but we were desperate. It was so terribly loud in here. It sounded like a freight train was rushing toward us as she charged closer. Her angry, skeletal face appeared in the doorway, a mass of darkness, a swirling shadow. A stench accompanied her that made it hard to breathe. We huddled together as the floor rattled beneath us. I could hear the dishes clattering in the cabinets in the kitchen. Cassidy was clutching both of my hands, and we were facing one another, praying together.

Cassidy was mumbling something about a light and trying to get her to the door, but that wasn't going to happen. Lynette had no desire to cross over, but this poor child needed me to do what she asked.

"Help me, Cassidy!" I dropped her hands and ran to the other side of the room. With all my might, I begin tugging on the mirror. It was secured to the wall, so there was no way to pull it down, but I did the next best thing. Cassidy must have been reading my mind because we both picked up knickknacks from around the room and began smashing the mirror.

We smashed the thing until there was no glass remaining. I cut myself more than once, but the job was done quickly.

And with our destruction of the mirror, we defeated Lynette.

We couldn't force her to leave, but she would no longer hold power here. All she could do was watch the living. But I wasn't going to allow her to have even that small victory. I stood up straight with a shard of glass in my hand and said, "You are banished, Lynette. You have no way to get back to where you were—the door is shut. You have to go. There is no place for you here—your hold is broken over Rebecca."

Even as I said the words, I saw wet footprints appearing on the floor. Rebecca was walking out of the room, into the kitchen and toward the back door. Before she disappeared, I heard a little moan, but at least she was gone from Brady Hall. I prayed to God she found peace wherever she went. We waited, I waited because I didn't believe that Lynette would be gone without more of a fight. Rebecca must have been the strong one. Without her to push around, to siphon energy from, Lynette couldn't manifest. She couldn't hurt anyone anymore. Ever again.

"It's over, Sierra Kay. It's all over." Cassidy hugged me, and together we cried with relief. I would probably have to pay for this mirror, but it was worth it. It was all worth it.

"Cassidy, don't call me that."

"What?" She stiffened in my arms. "Sorry, I just thought after all..."

"You have to call me Little Sister."

She smiled hugely as she led me out of the pile of mirror shards. "For real?" Her smile was beautiful and genuine.

"For real. Let's get out of here. I've got to buy some tanning oil. I need nothing but sun for the next week. After I take care of a few things at the office."

"Let's go, Little Sister."

We left Brady Hall and stepped out into the sunshine. I was happy to be among only the living. Out of the corner of my eye, I caught a glimpse of a sad little girl. She'd stay with me if I let her, but I shook my head.

I can't be your mommy. I have to raise my own daughter. Go, Rebecca. Love waits for you. It's calling you right now. Listen to it and follow.

And then she was gone.

I closed my eyes and let the sun warm my skin.

Yep. I liked being in the land of the living.

I think I'll stay here for a while.

Epilogue—Midas

"You want me to believe this garbage? How stupid do you think I am, Pete? After all this time, you want to come in here and tell me you are gay. Like that's an excuse for being such a lousy friend? You cheated on Jocelyn more times than I can count, and you left with Sara for Hollywood. Do you think I'm that stupid? You come out to me, and that's supposed to make it all better? That's crap, Peter Broadus. In fact, that's a new low, even for you."

"Being gay is crap?" Pete said in a serious tone.

"No. You're crap. That's what I mean. Now there you go. That's the Pete I know. Twist the words I say to make sure you look good in any situation." I was quickly losing my cool with my ex-friend. "I was wondering how long it would take before you became the victim. You're so good at that. You should really do a show about that." *Yeah, I was pretty damn furious at this point.* I slung a folder to the side and leaned on the desk, my hands clenched in tight fists. "Why don't you pitch that idea to your Hollywood guys? A hundred ways an ex-friend and paranormal investigator can be the victim—brought to you by the poster child for wannabe victims everywhere."

Peter's face paled at my sarcasm. "Do you hate me this much? You hate me so much that you can't listen to me when I'm telling you something that's very personal? I'm telling you I'm gay. It's not a trick, and it's not a ploy."

"And it's not an excuse for being a bad friend."

To that, he had no response at all, but I didn't feel bad for the guy. Not one little bit. I peered at him from across the desk and finally said, "Pete, you have shortcomings, but I never said being gay was among them. How could I? I never knew you were gay until now. Your sexuality is your own business, but it has nothing to do with you leaving us in the woods. That has nothing to do with you not showing up for Jocelyn's funeral. Being gay has nothing to do with all the lousy crap that you've done to us. And here's a question for you, Pete. If you're so gay, why did you fool around with Sierra? You took advantage of her. You knew that Joshua and Sierra were having problems, but you got all up in the middle of it. You could have broken them up for good. And for what? That's a sucky thing to do."

"I didn't force her to do it. She wanted to. I'm sure it was because she wanted to get back at Joshua, but I needed her too. It happened, and I can't take it back. We fooled around, but it was just the once. I guess more accurately that makes me bisexual, but does that matter?"

I was more than done with this guy. He had no remorse for any of his actions.

"You have been a lousy investigator and an even worse friend. Even if I believe you, it doesn't excuse anything you've done. What can you say to me that will excuse all of that?"

"Nothing. But I'm going to do something that I hope you approve of."

"Doubtful." I leaned back in the chair with my hands behind my head. My arms were sore from this morning's workout. "Leave the country? Move to another planet? The list of things I'd approve of is short, Pete, and you're wasting my time."

"You're such a smartass when you're mad. But I know you have every right to be mad." He sighed as he rubbed his eyes with his fingers. At least he was sober, and I didn't see any needle marks on his knuckles. "Look, I put myself in the worst situations ever. By being a drunk and by being an addict, I lowered my resistance to doing stupid things. I did take advantage of Sierra, and I encouraged your ex-girlfriend to make that move. I did all of those things. I did them all, but you have to know the truth about something. Sara and I never really you know...did the thing. She just wanted you to think so because she said that would be the only way she could get rid of you."

I think my jaw hit the floor. Pete took a deep breath and kept going, "I don't know how else to say that, but if I'm coming clean, I might as well come clean about everything. Sara had been unhappy for a long time, and she knew about me, Midas. I thought she would out me before I was ready. I wasn't ready. Not at all. Sara didn't have the courage to tell you that she wanted to leave, and I was foolish enough to believe she would leave without wrecking everything. I was a fool, Midas. My friendship with you means more to me than I could ever have expected or predicted. I ask you to forgive me. I ask you to give me another chance. Please?"

Well, this was a first. Pete never said "please" about anything. Was any of this true? Any of it at all? What was I going to do? Let him back in my life? No. That was not going to happen, but he was taking steps toward making his life better and I wanted to encourage him. Strangely enough, I could hear Sara's mocking voice in my ear.

Always a sucker for a sob story, Midas Demopolis.

"Peter, for whatever reason, I want you to be okay. I don't know why because I don't know which version of you is sitting in front of me. I don't know which version of the truth you're telling me, but I can honestly say that I'm never going to let you back on this team. Never. I can cheer you on from afar, but I'm not letting you back into Gulf Coast Paranormal. I wish you nothing but the best, but I think we're done here."

"I respect that, Midas. I figured as much, but I want you to know that I'm getting back into paranormal investigating. I'm starting my own group. I'd rather be with you guys, but since I can't be, since I've screwed that up, I want to at least be back in the field. Ghost work keeps me sane, and I was never happier than when I was working with Gulf Coast Paranormal. That's why I am starting my own group, not as competition but to help this area. The more the merrier, right? It's called Delta Hex Paranormal. We're going to be doing some investigations in Bayou La Batre, to begin with. I would love to collaborate with you on some projects and share data whenever the opportunity arises. I'm back in it, Midas. I'm back to doing what I love best."

"Don't get anyone killed, Pete. I wish you the best with your Delta Hex group. I have always wished you nothing but the best."

He appeared to breathe a sigh of relief. "I like the name. I'm working with Matt Hex. I decided not to put my name on the group, though. Delta was my idea. I feel like anything that had Broadus on it would certainly be doomed to fail. Anyway, thanks for listening to me. And thanks for understanding."

Pete rose from his chair awkwardly and stretched his hand out to me. "I'd like to part ways as friends this time," he said hopefully. "I'll try to stay out of your way, Midas."

I didn't agree with that and I didn't call him a friend, but I extended my hand as well. Papa Angelos always taught me that you shake a hand when it's presented to you. "I wish you the best, Pete. Thanks for stopping by."

With that, I watched my ex-best friend walk out of my office and followed him to the front to make sure he didn't bother Sierra on his way out. He wisely didn't speak a word to her but left quickly. That's when I noticed there was another guy in his vehicle. That must be that Hex character. What a strange last name. I silently prayed Peter knew what he was doing. And so did this Matt Hex.

Sierra asked, "Is he back?"

"No. He's never coming back."

She eyed me carefully. "No Helen, no Bruce. No Pete. Just the four of us. I guess we can handle it. Cassidy isn't quitting too, is she?"

I smiled at her. "Not a chance, as she's let me know in no uncertain terms. It's the four of us for now, but it's time," I said as I watched Pete and Matt Hex drive away.

"Time for what?" Sierra asked as she poked the pacifier in the baby's mouth. It was kind of nice having a baby in the office today.

"Time to bring in some new blood. Start sifting through the applications when you can, Sierra. No public posts, though; we don't want a bunch of rookies applying. Only professionals. I think it's time to kick up our game."

"Got it, Midas. In fact, there's a guy who's dying to meet you. His name is Ethan Wolfgang. He's been in New England, working mostly in Boston. He's a transplant and he's tremendously experienced. Should I set that up for today?"

"Wolfgang, huh? Well, with a name like that, he has to be interesting." I grinned at her and said, "There's no time like the present. Don't stop there, though. Ideally, I'd like to add four."

"Four? Really?"

"Yeah, really. And I want Joshua here full time. If he's comfortable with that."

Sierra was on her feet with tears in her eyes. "Really, Midas? Are you sure? You're not just screwing with me?"

"Nope. It's time to put my money where my mouth is, and that means taking care of the people I love. And trust. That's you and Joshua."

She hugged my neck and cried. "You don't know what this means to me."

"Yes, I do. But you're still taking that vacation. Make those appointments. I'll interview them all this week. And get Joshua in here to talk with me when he gets off work."

"Okay." She smiled as she stepped back behind her desk and picked up the phone. With her bare foot, she tilted the baby carrier to rock Emily.

Yeah, this was the right thing to do. I needed to put the past behind me. That included Jocelyn and Pete and Sara. Gulf Coast Paranormal was my future; the only thing that mattered was helping people. Cassidy and I agreed on that.

This was my life, and I loved it.

And here's the next Gulf Coast Paranormal investigation:

<u>THE GRAY LADY OF WILMER</u>[1]

---

1. https://www.amazon.com/dp/B083QQ16FG

Author's Note

Thank you so much for reading *The Spirits of Brady Hall*. I love lingering in the shadows of the spooky Gulf Coast! As some of you may know, this story first started on a lark because I was missing Ghost Hunters, but now, I can't imagine life without Midas, Sierra, Cassidy and Joshua. Every investigation, I learn something new about the field and my own local history. There's nothing like exploring haunted locations and calling it "work." I really, really love my job.

Brady Hall is a fictional name for an actual theater located in downtown Mobile. If you live here, it is the theater once used by Alabama Power for their downtown offices. It is reportedly haunted, and there was a murder there sometime in the early twentieth century. Apparently, it all happened right on stage, in front of the entire audience. Shocking, right? As always, I believe the ghost did it.

I enjoyed telling this story, and although it was difficult to uncover the actual details involving this love triangle, I tried to give all the players a voice.

If this is the first series of mine that you've read, please consider moving on to another one. The *Seven Sisters*[2] Series is a spooky journey down memory lane. If you prefer stories about darker hauntings, check out the *Sugar Hill*[3] Collection.

Want to be notified when my next book releases?Click here[4].

---

2.   *https://www.amazon.com/gp/product/*
   B081RL4BHH?ref_=dbs_dp_rwt_sb&binding=kindle_edition

3.   *https://www.amazon.com/gp/product/*
   B08CCYQL9J?ref_=dbs_dp_rwt_sb&binding=kindle_edition

Want to follow me on social media and see my writing progress? Eager to get peeks of my daily life and my embarrassingly extensive planner collection? I have you covered.

Follow me here: Facebook[5] —Twitter[6] —Instagram[7] —Website[8]

Thank you so much for purchasing this book. If you enjoyed it, please consider leaving a review or recommending me to a friend.

Thank you again for your support!

M.L. Bullock

---

4.   https://mlbullock.us11.list-manage.com/
subscribe?u=1e24b024a759e6520def3756b&id=df456e2598

5.   http://www.facebook.com/AuthorMLBullock

6.   https://twitter.com/AuthorMLBullock

7.   https://www.instagram.com/authormlbullock/

8.   http://www.mlbullock.com/

Don't miss out!

Visit the website below and you can sign up to receive emails whenever M.L. Bullock publishes a new book. There's no charge and no obligation.

https://books2read.com/r/B-A-CXMC-MRSTB

BOOKS 2 READ

Connecting independent readers to independent writers.

Also by M.L. Bullock

Desert Queen Saga
The Tale of Nefret
The Falcon Rises
The Kingdom of Nefertiti
The Song of the Bee Eater

Devecheaux Antiques and Haunted Things Trilogy Series
Devecheaux Antiques and Haunted Things
A Cup of Shadows
A Voice From Her Past
A Watch Of Weeping Angels

Gulf Coast Paranormal
The Ghosts of Kali Oka Road
The Ghosts of the Crescent Theater
A Haunting on Bloodgood Row
The Legend of the Ghost Queen
A Haunting at Dixie House

The Ghost Lights of Forrest Field
The Ghost of Gabrielle Bonet
The Ghost of Harrington Farm
The Creature on Crenshaw Road
A Ghostly Ride in Gulfport
The Ghosts of Phoenix No.7
The Maelstrom of the Leaf Academy
The Ghosts of Oakleigh House
The Spirits of Brady Hall
The Gray Lady of Wilmer

Gulf Coast Paranormal Season Two
The Beast of Limerick House

Gulf Coast Paranormal Trilogy Series
Ghosted
Haunted
Dead
Spooked
Paranormal

Haunting Passions
For the Love of Shadows

Idlewood
The Ghosts of Idlewood
Dreams of Idlewood
The Whispering Saint
The Haunted Child

Marietta
The Bones of Marietta
Footsteps of Angels

Return to Seven Sisters
The Roses of Mobile
All the Summer Roses
Blooms Torn Asunder
A Garden of Thorns
Wreath of Roses

Scary Fall Stories
Horrible Little Things

Seven Sisters
Seven Sisters

Moonlight Falls On Seven Sisters
Shadows Stir At Seven Sisters
The Stars That Fell
The Stars We Walked Upon
The Sun Rises Over Seven Sisters
Beyond Seven Sister
Ghost on a Swing

Sugar Hill
Wife Of The Left Hand
Fire On The Ramparts
Blood By Candlelight
The Starlight Ball
His Lovely Garden

Summerleigh
The Belles of Desire, Mississippi
The Ghost Of Jeoprady Belle
The Lady In White
Loxley Belle

Twelve to Midnight
Mary Twelves

About the Author

Author M.L. Bullock enjoys the laid-back atmosphere and the spooky vibe of the Gulf Coast, especially the region's historic districts and sites. When she isn't visiting her favorite haunts in New Orleans or Old Mobile, you can find her flipping through old photographs or newspaper clippings in search of new inspiration.

Read more at www.mlbullock.com.